W9-AZK-180

MY NAME IS

Henry Bibb

A STORY OF SLAVERY AND FREEDOM

Messing Library
Mary Institute &
St. Louis Country Day School
101 North Warson
St. Louis, Missouri 63124

MY NAME IS

Henry Bibb

A STORY OF

Slavery

AND

Freedom

Afua Cooper

KCP FICTION
An Imprint of Kids Can Press

To my son Akil and grandson Jahnoi

KCP Fiction is an imprint of Kids Can Press

Text © 2009 Afua Cooper

All rights reserved. No part of this publication may be reproduced, stored in a
retrieval system or transmitted, in any form or by any means, without the prior
written permission of Kids Can Press Ltd. or, in case of photocopying or other
reprographic copying, a license from The Canadian Copyright Licensing Agency
(Access Copyright). For an Access Copyright license, visit www.accesscopyright.ca
or call toll free to 1-800-893-5777.

Kids Can Press acknowledges the financial support of the Government of Ontario,
through the Ontario Media Development Corporation's Ontario Book Initiative;
the Ontario Arts Council; the Canada Council for the Arts; and the Government
of Canada, through the BPIDP, for our
publishing activity.

Published in Canada by	Published in the U.S. by
Kids Can Press Ltd.	Kids Can Press Ltd.
25 Dockside Drive	2250 Military Road
Toronto, ON M5A 0B5	Tonawanda, NY 14150

www.kidscanpress.com

Edited by Charis Wahl
Designed by Marie Bartholomew

Manufactured in Altona, Manitoba, Canada, in 10/2010 by Friesens Corporation

This book is printed on acid-free paper that is 100% ancient-forest friendly
(100% post-consumer recycled).

CM 09 0 9 8 7 6 5 4 3 2

Library and Archives Canada Cataloguing in Publication

Cooper, Afua
        My name is Henry Bibb : a story of slavery and
freedom / written by Afua Cooper.

ISBN 978-1-55337-813-6

1. Bibb, Henry, b. 1815—Juvenile fiction. 2. Slaves—United States—
Biography—Juvenile fiction. 3. Abolitionists—United States—Biography—
Juvenile fiction. 4. African Americans— Biography—Juvenile fiction. I. Title.

PS8555.O584M9 2009   jC813'.54   C2008-907591-9

Kids Can Press is a *l*©*∩*s™ Entertainment company

Prologue

MY NAME IS HENRY BIBB. I WAS BORN A SLAVE.
THIS WAS IN SHELBY COUNTY, KENTUCKY, IN 1814.
MY MOTHER'S NAME IS MILDRED JACKSON, AND
SHE TOO WAS A SLAVE. MY MOTHER HAD SEVEN
SONS, ALL OF WHOM WERE FATHERED BY SLAVE-
HOLDERS. MY FATHER IS JAMES BIBB, A MEMBER OF
THE WHITE SLAVEHOLDING CLASS. BUT ALL I GOT
FROM HIM WAS HIS NAME AND COMPLEXION.

By the time I was ten I was hired out to various
slaveholders, most of whom abused me to the point
of near death. Under these regimes of torment, I
resolved to escape. I ran away for brief periods but
was always found and brought back.

As I grew older I came to understand that slavery was meant to crush its victim, drive him mad,
render him a thing incapable of fighting back,
and accepting of his lot.

When I became a young man, I married and
fathered a daughter. The birth of our child made
me realize that the time had come for me to make
a bid for liberty. I would escape and then return to
free my family.

CHAPTER ONE

Sold Before I Was Born

My mother's walk was heavy and lumbering, though she breathed deeply. Some days were filled with a complete and thorough silence that seeped into everything around me. Awed by this deep silence, I stopped moving. Other days, there was noise and activity. Still, my mother could not do much, other than repeat again and again, "Help me, Lord." In the slowness of her body, I could feel myself groping toward something new. I would leave my home of water and darkness. I would go into another world.

One early morning in May, I pushed myself into that world. My mother cried, and I did too. But she held me, hushed me and stroked my skin. The midwife bathed me in warm water scented with lemongrass and wrapped me up. My mother held me to her bosom and nursed me. The light hurt my eyes so I kept them closed. I was drowsy, lulled by my mother's cooing and the warmth of her body. Then I heard her say, "Listen, little one,

I have a story to tell you." I suddenly grew alert. "You are as beautiful as the sun." Then she began, in a sad but sweet voice.

"Once a group of Africans came to America. They were Ibos. They came off the ship, their hands and feet shackled. As they came onto the land, they realized that a life of slavery lay in store for them. So they turned around, every last one of them — children, women and men — and walked into the sea. Even when their feet could no longer touch bottom, they kept on going until they reached Africa. Those Africans knew how to walk on water. One day, my son, you too will leave all this behind."

I had no idea what my mother was talking about. Water I knew, because I had been living in it for nine months. But who were Africans and what was America? What was slavery? One thing I sensed, and it was that the Africans knew that in America their life would be unbearable. So they left. After the story my mother hummed and rocked me. She lay beside me on the mat and held me close. Soon, we were both asleep.

On 14 May 1814, I was born. My mother, Mildred, an enslaved mulatto woman, named me Henry. Her master, Richard Butler, added Walton as my middle name. My last name was that of my father, a free White man named James Bibb. According to the law, any child born of a slave woman was also a slave. I was born mostly White, but part Black and therefore a slave. When I was about eight years old, my mother told me that my father had died when I was three. Not that it mattered. He never claimed me as his child. White men had their way with slave women, their own and others, but took no notice of the consequences. My mother was one such woman.

Instead of a father, I had sorrow. My mother was owned by a man named Robert Hunter. When she became pregnant with me a planter named Richard Butler bought her for four hundred dollars. She was seventeen years old. While my mother worked in Butler's house and waited for me to be born, Butler's daughter, Sophia, married David White. By the time I was born and nursing, Sophia was pregnant, but died giving birth to a daughter. Richard Butler grieved for his beloved daughter and felt keen sorrow for his baby granddaughter. Motherless, Harriet needed someone to provide milk for her. In those days, it was common practice for slave women who were nursing their own children to nurse White babies as well.

Butler gave my mother to his infant granddaughter as a gift. He drew up a deed giving Harriet "one Negro woman named Milly and her infant son Henry, and the future increase of said Milly." Harriet White, a baby, owned me and my mother. Should my mother give birth to other children, Harriet would also own them.

My mother lived in David White's house and became his housekeeper. I lived with her. When I was older, she told me that she used to feel that both children were hers, not just the one she gave birth to. She would hold both of us at her bosom and nurse us. When I understood the vileness that was slavery, I realized that Harriet White not only stole my mother's labor but also my milk.

Our master, David White, was a tall, burly man with a mop of red hair that kept falling in his eyes. His skin was pasty white. He owned a modest farm in Shelby County, in the bluegrass area of

Kentucky. The farm was blessed with a large expanse of prairie lands interspersed with undulating hills. The property bordered one of the principal county roads, and a sizable river ran at the base of the land. About twenty slave people grew corn, tobacco, indigo, hemp and various vegetables. They also raised pigs and goats for the slaughterhouses of Ohio and Indiana. Our nearest neighbor was about four miles away.

David White was a government lawyer and spent much time in the Kentucky state capital, Frankfort. Because he was away for long periods he hired a manager, a vicious, bowlegged man named Captain Barker. It was said that Barker had fought in the War of 1812. He took great pleasure in whipping the slaves, although when I was young I was spared because I was Harriet White's playmate. Yet, when he passed me in the yard, he would screw up his eyes, spew tobacco juice at me and mutter, "One day, Henry, I will get you."

Harriet and I, because we were the only children in the big house, grew up together. I cannot remember my early life without Harriet, and came to think that she was my sister. As we grew we played outside under a huge oak that stood in the front yard of the house. Harriet and I would hold hands, and she would say, "Come on, Henry, my little nigger." When I was about seven years old, I asked my mother what Harriet meant by "nigger." She was peeling potatoes.

"Mama, what is a nigger?"

"Where did you hear that?"

"Harriet called me her 'little nigger.'"

My mother's eyes filled with tears and pain.

"Never mind Harriet," she said. "A 'nigger' is what White people call us slaves."

"What is a slave?"

"A slave is someone that another person owns. You and me. Sister Dinah, Shadrach, Lucy, Old Trevor — all of us who work for Mr. White — are slaves. The Black people."

"But I am White, Mother. You are, too."

My mother laughed out loud. She pulled me to her and hugged me. "You *look* White. And I have enough White blood in me to look White, too. But the blood of Africa in our veins makes us Black.

"Henry, Harriet owns us. Her grandfather owned us and gave us to her. She is our owner, though this is her father's house and plantation."

I became quite dizzy. What I had just learned filled me with such surprise that all I could do was sit and listen to my breath going in and out.

"Listen, Henry," my mother whispered. "When you were born I told you a story about the Ibos, the Africans, the Black people who could walk on water and how they walked right back to Africa."

I did not remember such a story but nodded nonetheless.

"Africans could also fly." My mother must have seen doubt in my eyes because she said, "It is true. My own mother told me. Once upon a time, Africans could fly."

"Why can't they fly now?"

"The White people threw salt at their feet."

"What?"

"Those who never forgot Africa, who held it close to their hearts, whose spirits never gave in to slavery used to go down to the riverside. Some would beat rhythms on drums and, like magic, those who wanted to go home would rise up into the air and fly away. But others, those whose spirits slavery had broken, learned what was happening, and they told the White people. One day, as some Africans prepared to fly away, patrollers seized them and sprinkled salt at their feet. It is said that salt makes people so heavy that they remain bound to the earth. But even today, some of us still fly away. Every day, Henry, slaves vanish into thin air and massa never finds them. Don't worry about Miss Harriet. One day you will be like those Africans and fly away."

CHAPTER TWO

Hired Out

By the time I was eight years old, I was working as a household domestic. I helped my mother with the scrubbing and polishing of the floors. I learned how to peel and scrape potatoes, to shell peas, help with the food preparation and dust furniture. I also gathered firewood with other slave children. Though I still played with Harriet, I could not spend as much time doing so because of my work. My master also discouraged us from playing together. He did not think it wise for a free White girl to be playing with a Black slave boy. Further, Harriet had begun her education. A tutor named Simmons, a Yankee man, came to the house every day to instruct her in reading and writing.

As my master grew successful as a lawyer and planter, he wished to increase his domestic staff to show his increasing prosperity. Mr. White brought guests whenever he came to stay in the country, and my poor mother would work around the clock to satisfy their every need. She must have complained because one day he returned home from Frankfort with a mulatto slave named Suzette to take over the cooking.

My mother rejoiced at Suzette's arrival. Now she could get some respite both from her duties and from Mr. White. (During the eight years we had been living at his farm, my mother had given birth to two more boys, George and John. I was four years older than George and six years older than John.) When Suzette arrived, my mother asked David White for her own cabin in the slave quarter. While we lived in the house, my mother and we three boys had slept on the floor in Harriet's bedroom. Now Harriet would have Suzanne with her in the house, and my mother could have her privacy.

Living in her own cabin did not mean she ceased working as a maid in Mr. White's house. Every morning before dawn I accompanied her to the house, then returned to the cabin to look after my brothers and give them breakfast.

Suzette became a sister to my mother, and loved us with all her heart. When I first saw her I thought she would be unfriendly, as she had a mournful countenance and walked with her head bowed. But she looked up at me and smiled. After that, every time she saw me or my brothers she would hug us close. She did this many times a day. And she was forever giving us sweets, cakes and roast meat. Though I was glad for the attention, I was puzzled by it. I asked my mother why Suzette loved us so.

"Massa White bought her from a slave dealer in Lexington. She had two boy children who looked just like you and your brothers; but when she was sold to Massa White, her sons were sold to a planter from Tennessee," my mother said. "Her husband was sold to Alabama. She grieves that she will never see them again."

One day I was stoning the leaves off the big oak tree that stood in the front yard when I saw Simmons, the tutor, mount his horse and ride away. That signalled that Harriet would have afternoon refreshment.

"Let's play a game." The voice belonged to Harriet.

Startled, I looked around and shook my head slowly.

"Don't feel like it," I said.

"Henry, you are my nigger and you must do as I tell you," she said in the voice that she used whenever she wanted to have her way.

I glowered at Harriet, wanting to tell her that I was not her nigger.

"Africans can fly, and one day I will."

"What are you talking about, Henry? You ain't an African, and you sure cannot fly."

I stared at Harriet, my anger rising.

"Come here, boy."

Harriet and I both turned at the sound of the voice. It belonged to Shadrach, the blacksmith. Shadrach spent most of his time around fire, melting metals, hammering out utensils, horseshoes and tools for the field. Working at the forge made Shadrach's eyes red, and must have burnt all the fat from his body. Shadrach had a cabin right behind his smithy, yet day and night he might be found in his shop working metal.

His ways were mysterious. You could be walking on the farm, and out of nowhere he would appear. It was as if he emerged from the trees or from the very earth itself. Once, when I was picking berries, I sensed a presence behind me. Startled, I turned around. Shadrach merely said, "Sorry Henry, I was gathering herbs," and walked in the opposite direction.

He learned his trade from his father. In Africa, his father had been a smith, and when he came to America he fetched a high price for his skills. His father had also been a smith, and his father's father before him. Smiths were important people in Africa, not only for their trade, but because it was said they possessed magic. They were great hunters who could talk to the plants and animals, and were also skilled herbalists.

Massa David prized Shadrach very highly: not only did Shadrach work for him, but he also worked for other planters and for the racetrack in Louisville. During the racing season Massa moved Shadrach to Louisville so he could work unhindered, making shoes for the horses. He made lots of money for our master, who had agreed that Shadrach would keep a portion of his wages.

Shadrach always seemed to think deeply about his words before he spoke them. His voice was gruff, yet he was kind, especially to the children, giving them fruit and sweet cakes. He had no wife or children, yet he seemed satisfied in his aloneness.

He said again, "Come here, boy."

I walked over to where Shadrach stood. "Don't say that kind of stuff to Miss Harriet. And if she wants to play with you, then play with her." Then he stooped to match his height with mine, and said in a half-whisper, "Play with Miss Harriet, just don't tell her any of the things your mother told you. You will put us all in danger. If you were meant to fly, you will. If you were meant to walk on water, you will. You understand, boy?"

I nodded my head.

"Good."

Shadrach then continued on his way. As he passed her, he lifted his hat and said, "Good day, Miss Harriet."

My mother then appeared on the porch, George and John on either side. John tugged at her skirt, and she picked him up.

I remember when my mother went into labor with him. It was summer and the sun was already high in the sky. My mother and I were in the drawing room dusting the furniture. She placed one hand over her belly and let out a long sigh.

"Mama, are you all right?"

"Go tell Shadrach to bring Sister Dinah," she said. "Hurry."

I could hear the pounding of Shadrach's hammer as I ran down to the smithy. "Mama said to get Sister Dinah." Without saying a word, Shadrach put down his tools and drove off in the wagon.

When he came back with Sister Dinah, my mother was in our cabin. The midwife sent me and George outside. After what seemed a long time she called us in. My mother was lying with a baby, as red as a beet, in her arms.

I opened his fist and placed my finger in his palm. He held my finger. George kissed the baby on his forehead.

Now seeing my brothers standing with our mother, I felt a sadness in my heart for all of us fatherless souls.

———

Maybe Harriet told her father about what I had said about Africans flying, I do not know. But, soon afterward, David White summoned my mother, and she was instructed to bring me along with her.

She held my hand as we walked toward our master's study.

We found David White seated at his desk, poring over notes. He looked up and adjusted his glasses.

"Milly, it concerns Henry. I am going to hire him out. He spends most of his time doing nothing."

"He helps me in the house, Massa, and sometimes he helps Shadrach." My mother's hand gripped mine tightly, and her breath came fast.

"I've hired him out, Milly. The boy is almost ten. It's time he engaged in useful work. The contract is already signed." But David White did not need to explain his actions. He owned us body and soul. Hiring out of slaves was a common practice in Kentucky for two main reasons: if owners believed their slaves had not enough work, or if owners were in need of money.

I felt my blood grow cold. Hire out? I knew what that meant. Old Trevor had been hired out many times, and each time he came back to the farm emaciated, weak and ill. Now Old Trevor was no use to himself. He just sat at the door of his cabin fanning flies. Hire out meant that I would be away from my mother and brothers. I felt tears spring to my eyes.

"I don't want to go, Massa."

"It's all right, Henry." My mother tried to soothe me.

"Get the boy ready. He leaves immediately."

"Lord have mercy, Massa! Can't he leave tomorrow?"

"Get the boy ready, Milly. He leaves now."

When we got outside, I saw the tears running down my mother's face. We walked in silence to our cabin, where she packed my few things in a cloth bag and began preparing some food. I looked around the cabin: the fireplace with the pots and pans and eating bowls stacked to one side, the sleeping mats rolled up against the wall, the pine table and four stools that Justice, the carpenter, had made. I would miss all of it.

My mother was making a gumbo, corn flour mixed with vegetables and bits of meat. This was a treat, because I was leaving.

"Go fetch your brothers," she told me.

I left the cabin with a heavy heart to go to Hannah's place. Hannah was an old slave woman who tended the younger children on the plantation. Soon I returned with John and George. John had been sleeping, so I carried him home and sat with him on my lap.

"Where am I going?" I asked my mother.

"Don't know. Will have to ask him."

She shared the food in silence. John awakened and began to cry. I soothed him, cooled some gumbo and spooned it into his mouth. He ate greedily. I had no appetite. After I fed him, I felt drowsy and fell asleep.

I was awakened by the sound of a neighing horse.

"Wake up, Henry. Massa is here," my mother called.

I roused myself and held John close. I kissed him on his forehead. "Don't worry, I will be back in no time."

George stood silent beside the fireplace. "When you coming back, Henry?"

"Soon, soon. And I will bring back something nice for you."

My mother was outside the cabin door, my bag in her hand. She hugged me. "There is some roast meat and corn bread in the bag, and also a bottle of ginger beer. Remember now, Henry, behave yourself." Then she stooped and said for my ears alone to hear, "And remember the stories about the old Africans."

A few yards from the cabin, my master got down

from his horse and walked over to Shadrach, who was waiting with a wagon, and gave him a piece of paper. Several boys and girls sat in the wagon. Like me, they were being hired out.

My master said, "Shadrach, take Henry to Widow Beverly. Milly, I need you in the house now."

Shadrach clicked his tongue and the horse moved off. I sat with my back to the farm. I could not bear to see my mother going into my master's house to provide for his pleasure.

***

Boxer, Shadrach's dog, ran behind the wagon, barking. He had become a pet of mine. I fed him, bathed him in the creek and spent many happy times roaming the woods with him on our plantation. But the horse was too fast. Soon we lost sight of him, and his bark grew faint.

A slight breeze caressed our faces as the wagon slogged along the county road. The night before there had been a big downpour, and the road was filled with puddles and pools of water that turned it to mud. Sometimes the wheels of the wagon got stuck. The poor horse would complain with loud neighs. Shadrach would have to get down, put his

Messing Library
Mary Institute &
Saint Louis Country Day School
101 North Warson
St. Louis, Missouri 63124

shoulders to the wagon's back and push with all his might.

The countryside was still coming to life with the spring, and the trees boasted new leaves. Wildflowers sprang up by the wayside. The sun had started to sink behind the distant trees, and the day took on a dreamy quality. Suddenly, Shadrach began to sing. The song was not in English. I imagined it was in the language of his African ancestors. Shadrach often told of how his grandfather was a true-born African. It was a spirited song, and Shadrach moved his body in big circles as he sang.

As if summoned, a swarm of butterflies with purple wings dotted with red and white descended on us. It was as if someone had opened up a multi-colored blanket and covered us with it. We all squealed with delight and tried catching the butterflies. The entire road was filled with them, and they let out a low sound like bumblebees.

"Whoa, whoa," Shadrach called out to the horse. He pulled on the reins and stopped the wagon. He also stopped his singing and gazed at the butterflies with a big grin on his face. "So beautiful, so beautiful," he said, over and over.

"There's a certain plant that grows here in abundance. It collects water and makes a sweet drink that this type of butterfly likes. That is why there are so many of them here," Shadrach explained.

A few moments later, the butterflies left us with the same speed and suddenness with which they had descended. They formed a single line and in perfect order fluttered higher in the air and disappeared. The beauty of what I had just witnessed and lost filled me with such a bitter longing that I burst into a loud lament. The other children turned to look at me, and they too began to wail.

"Now, now, now," Shadrach said. He jumped from his seat, dug his hand into his pocket and pulled out a fold of cloth. He opened it and took out small yellowish lumps. "Here, each of you, take one. It is sugar. Grown far away, in a place called Grenada."

With tears still running down our cheeks and snot oozing from our nostrils, we each took a sugar lump and placed it on our tongue. At the farm, only the White people had sugar. The slave people used honey. So how did Shadrach get sugar? I pushed the thought from my mind and willed the sweetness on my tongue to last.

"It will be all right. You will see your mammies again soon."

Day was speeding toward night when the wagon pulled up at a stately house. Shadrach jumped from his seat and walked briskly to the veranda, calling my name. The butler opened the door. I jumped from the wagon.

"This here boy is Henry," Shadrach said. "He is Widow Beverly's personal servant."

"Go around to the kitchen. Maude will look after him," was all the butler said, and shut the door in our faces.

After a few attempts we found the kitchen and Maude. A slimmer person I had never seen in my life. Did this woman eat only air? After Shadrach explained me to Maude he had to leave to deliver the other children to their new places of work. But he placed both his hands on my shoulders, stooped to look in my eyes, and said, "Take care, Henry, and remember the stories your mama told you. Keep them always in your heart." And with that he was gone.

"It's late now. Widow does not like to be disturbed," Maude said. "I will take you to see her tomorrow."

I looked up at her, sleep in my eyes. "You will sleep here tonight."

"Where?" I looked around the kitchen.

Maude opened a door to a small room. On the floor was a pallet. "Here."

⟨ornament⟩

The Widow Beverly lived in Henry County, some miles from the town of Newcastle. She was called "widow" on account of the death of her first husband. Although her second husband was a government surveyor and spent long periods away from home, the widow had the company of her five-year-old son, Nathan. Her plantation was smaller than my master's, but her slaves did the same kind of work. However, she used a slave to supervise his fellow slaves, and to do the general overseeing of the farm. He was known as a slave driver.

I quickly discovered that when God was giving out lazy the widow was at the head of the line. Rahel, one of the female servants, ran the widow's bath, bathed her and helped her dress, then brought her breakfast, which she ate in bed with Nathan. Then she sat all day on the porch in her lounge chair. Summer came quickly to our part of Kentucky, and May brought with it summer's heat. While the widow viewed the activities of the farm, my job was to fan her and bring lemonade. I fanned till my hands hurt and my eyes became heavy. Sometimes I fell asleep while fanning, only to be slapped into consciousness by the widow. "Lazy boy, wake up!" She left the porch only to have her luncheon and dinner.

I combed and added pomade to her hair, and brushed it until my arm ached. I also tended to her fingernails and toenails. Sometimes my ten-year-old fingers slipped and the tiny scissors poked one of her fingers, drawing blood. She would then fly into a rage and box me all over my face. Once, only the intervention of one of the house servants saved me from certain death.

I was also the widow's skin-care doctor. Pimples often appeared on her face, and I was to burst them. Entire mornings were spent bursting Widow Beverly's pimples. If I squeezed her skin too hard, she would box and kick me.

Even though Widow Beverly was the laziest woman, she constantly criticized the house servants.

Rahel was mainly responsible for tidying the house and serving the meals; but the house was never clean enough for the widow. Sometimes she would leave her chair on the porch, walk to the dining or drawing room and run her fingers across a table or cabinet. "Rahel!" she would scream, and the unfortunate girl would come running. "Is this dust that I see here?"

"I will wipe it away right now, ma'am," Rahel would say as she attempted to side-step the widow. But she was never fast enough. The widow would hit her across the head. Once I saw her grab the hem of Rahel's dress to wipe a side table. "Next time I will use your hair!" she yelled.

Nor did Elliot, the butler, escape the widow's wrath. His duties included polishing the silver and cleaning her shoes, and she always found fault. She would go to the side table where the silver was kept. If it was not shined to her liking, and sometimes even if it was, she would order Elliot to polish everything again. He stayed away from her as best as he could.

Sometimes it was clear that the devil possessed the widow. Oftentimes I would be fanning her and she would suddenly jump from the chair and bolt into the kitchen.

"Are you stealing my ham again?" she'd shout to Maude. "I get this distinct feeling that you are eating my ham, Maude."

Maude would not say a word but would stare down at the widow with her aristocratic gaze. Widow Beverly could not bear Maude's gaze.

"You answer me when I am talking to you, girl!"

Once, Maude did answer. "I do not eat pork, ma'am."

For once, Widow Beverly was at a loss for words. She fled to the porch and yelled, "Henry, come rub my feet."

The house servants ate in the kitchen, after the widow and Nathan had been served their meals. Maude had to serve us small portions, as it was the custom of our mistress to appear in the kitchen unexpectedly to see what was on our plates. One evening she told Maude she was giving me too much food and that I didn't deserve it since I was so lazy. After that Maude lessened my portions; but when it was time for bed, she took from the larder bits of roast chicken, corn bread and baked potatoes and gave them to me without saying a word. She just sat and watched me eat, and when I was finished she patted my arm.

The other slaves in the house said Maude was descended from royalty on both the White and Black sides of her family. One of her grandmothers was an African princess; her grandfather was fathered by the Duke of Cornwall. This duke had come to America, set up a plantation and begun a family with one of his female slaves. Like my father, he never acknowledged any of those children as his own, but kept them in bondage.

Maude did carry herself like royalty. She spoke only when necessary, did not mix with the other slaves and held herself erect. But beneath that stern exterior was a kind heart — at least for me. She rarely showed her emotions, but she treated me well and warned me when I was in danger from my mistress's temper. I wondered if Maude had any children, but her stern visage prevented me from asking.

I noticed that all the slaves who worked in the house were of my complexion. Not one was dark-skinned. Elliot, the butler, was like me, almost white. Maude was a mulatto, like my mother, as was Rahel. Years later I would come to know that some Whites did not want dark-skinned Blacks to work in their homes. Unmixed Blacks were "too foreign." Perhaps a black, black skin frightened them. It would have been better if it made them feel guilty. Sadly, I would discover that many Black people shared this preference, having learned well the slaveholders' prejudice that whiter is better. Some house slaves were also related to the slaveholders. Perhaps that was one reason that house slaves were better clothed than those who worked in the fields. House slaves, too, often wore shoes.

I looked back over my time at the widow's as a period of almost unending misery. Each day, I was beaten, boxed or kicked. Seeing no end to my intolerable existence, one day after a severe beating I ran away. I did not plan to, but after the beating, the forest that bordered the house looked so inviting I walked toward it. Then, I ran. I ran and ran and ran. There was enough daylight for me to see that the woods was a pleasant place. A small river ran through it, and past the river was a hill that commanded a good view of the surrounding area. I immersed myself in the water and felt the pain and anger drain from me. After my bath, I found some berries for my supper. I remained for three days in the woods until some field slaves sent by the widow found me and brought me back to the house; and she soon went back to her evil ways.

I became very good at running. Whenever the widow took to punching and kicking me, I would take off. Sometimes I would be gone for a few days. I stayed in the woods and lived off the land. Sometimes I would carry a horse's harness with me in case someone discovered me. At least twice I was surprised by White men on horses. Each time they looked at me intently and asked, "Boy, you a runaway?"

"No, Massa," I answered. "My mistress's horse took off, and I am looking for it." Seeing the harness, they believed the story and rode away.

<hr />

Fall came and with it cooler weather. It was the time of harvest. Though the widow did not approve of house slaves socializing with those who worked in the field, I would go down to the slave quarters whenever my work allowed, and I quickly got to know the slave folks who lived there. One evening in late October, I went to play with a boy my age named David. The adults were preparing for a corn-shucking. David and I walked out to the cornfields with them. Shucking corn was work but also a time of merrymaking, and the sociability made the work seem lighter. Slaves from neighboring farms would join in the harvest, moving between farms to pick and store the crops.

Slaveowners gave permission for the shucking, but it was the slave people who organized it. About fifty slaves assembled at the cornfield, and Winston, the Widow Beverly's slave driver, gave them all whisky to encourage them to work as fast as they could. Then they chose captains and divided themselves into three groups. Each group would try to shuck its row of corn faster than the other two. As the men and women broke down the dried cornstalks, removed the outer leaves of the corn, took the corn from its stalk, removed the silk and then threw the corn in wooden bins at the end of each path, they lifted their voices in song. The captain called and his workers answered.

Captain: Fare you well, Miss Lucy

All: John come down to de hollow

Captain: Fare you well, fare you well

All: well ooh, well ooh

Captain: Fare you well, young ladies all

All: Well ooh, well ooh

Captain: Fare you well all, I'm going away

All: Well ooh, well ooh

Captain: I'm going away to Canada

All: Well ooh, well ooh!

The song had a mournful air even though the people sang it with powerful voices. I knew the song well but had never really paid attention to the words. Now, as the people sang, I heard "I'm going away to Canada" as if for the first time. The words went around in my head. But what is Canada? It must be a place, but where? I knew of Tennessee, Ohio, Indiana and such, but I did not know of that place. I asked David, but he did not know either.

That night as I helped Elliot polish the silver, I asked him.

"Where did you hear that, boy?" he asked harshly.

"From the corn-shucking song."

"Oh," he said, and remained quiet for a while. Then he said, "It's a free place way up north. Another country, not America. They have a king. They speak English like us. Many slave people from Kentucky go there."

"Ohio and Indiana are free places," I ventured.

"Yes, but a massa can still go there and capture runaways. It's safer to head straight to Canada." Elliot stopped polishing and looked off into space. After a while, he added, "Or Mexico."

"Where is that?"

"Way south. They speak Spanish there."

"But there is no slavery there?"

"No."

"How do you get there?"

"Mexico?"

"No, Canada."

"You cross the Ohio River to a free state and keep on very far north." Elliot took up his polishing rag again but looked directly at me. "Now, Henry, don't go asking too many questions, you hear?

Don't let the widow ever find you know what I just told you."

From that moment I had one dream: to cross the Ohio and head north. The corn shucking, that one bright spot in the blanket of regret and grief with which I was covered at the widow's, gave me knowledge of a world of freedom beyond the slavery in which I languished.

⸺⸺⸺

On my last day at the widow's she was in the drawing room, as it had grown too cool for the porch. She ordered me to bring her chair close to the fireplace; then, of course, she complained she was too hot, so I had to fan her. Her tall glass of lemonade sparkled on a side table. Suddenly, the widow jumped from her chair, mumbling about her food being stolen in the kitchen. She barged into me, knocked me down and stepped over my prostrate body. I could not get up as I felt dizzy, then drowsy, and soon fell asleep. I was awakened by shouting and something hitting my ribs. It was the widow's foot. "Look what you did!" she was shrieking, and pointed to the lemonade. Black ants had covered the glass. I felt the *thud, thud* of her shoes in my back, belly and chest. I curled up, holding my hands over my face, so that her kicks would not blind me. My heart raged against Widow Beverly and I thought of all the ways I could get back at her, even burning down her house with her in it.

But it was Elliot who saved me.

"Widow Beverly, careful, ma'am." Elliot lifted me from the floor and held me against his body. "Henry here is a hire. If he was your'n, you could do what you wished, but ..." His voice trailed off.

"Send him back to David White."

"Yes'm."

Before I left she had Maude bathe and oil me to disguise the marks from the blows she had inflicted. But it was not me she cared about. She was afraid of my master's anger at damaging his property. And I was valuable. Elliot told me that my master had hired me to the widow for one hundred dollars a year. My master was earning one hundred dollars for my labor. And I earned nothing but beatings.

A field hand walked me the ten miles from the widow's farm to David White's plantation. I could not have been happier.

CHAPTER THREE

Back at My Old Master's

Boxer announced my arrival. I heard his loud barking at least a mile from David White's plantation. As soon as he saw me, he bounded over and then threw himself into my arms. I rubbed his ears and embraced him. Some of the plantation people came to see what was going on.

My mother cried when she saw me. "I had no idea you were coming today." Boxer eased himself from my arms and my mother scooped me up. "Oh my God, you have grown so big."

"Why are you back, boy?" David White stood tapping his riding whip on his leg.

The field hand answered for me. "The widow said she does not need his services anymore. She prefers to be served by a female, Massa, and she sends this letter. I better be off, Massa, before it gets dark." He handed the letter to David White and walked briskly from the yard.

David White looked at me and my mother. "You may take him to your cabin, Milly, but tomorrow I want him in the house for work."

"I have a surprise for you," my mother said as we walked toward her cabin.

"A good one?"

"Yes."

When we got to our small house, my brothers were asleep and so was the surprise — a new baby, born while I was away at the widow's.

"Tell me about you. How have you been?" my mother asked, as she peered at me.

I wanted to tell her "fine," but the word would not come out of my mouth. "I missed you all so much," was what I managed to say.

"How did you get that bruise across your face?"

"From the widow."

"Come here, Henry."

My mother took off my shirt.

"Oh my God, how did you get these?" she asked, running her hands over my bruised and battered skin. I remained quiet. "It was the widow?"

I nodded.

My mother heated water, prepared a bath and filled

it with all kinds of soothing leaves. She commanded me to sit in it as she prepared supper. How happy I was to be home.

As night deepened, visitors came. First Shadrach, then Dinah the midwife, and later Pearl with her three children. They all commented on how much I had grown and said that now I was a real man to have been hired out and all. Shadrach asked if I remembered my mother's stories. I nodded, though in truth I had not thought of them at the widow's.

"Don't full up the boy's head with nonsense," Pearl said to Shadrach.

"What stories?"

"Stories about Africans who could fly and walk on water." Pearly sucked her teeth loudly. "Shadrach, you are a fool. If they could do all those miracles, why are we still here and under Captain Barker's bullwhip, Milly, tell me that?"

"It don't mean directly they could fly or walk on water, Pearl," my mother said. "It means that they had powers to hide themselves from massa, to make themselves invisible."

"Henry, boy," Pearl said, "you are your mother's

eldest child, and so you must be wise. Take my advice, don't listen to any of this foolishness."

My mother steered the talk to the harvest.

Before I set to work in my master's house he gave me a talking to. He said that though the widow did not tell him, he knew I had become a runaway. "Things like that are not kept hidden, boy." He then warned me that if I tried to escape from his plantation, he would sell me down the river. "I know that your mother wants to have you close, and I like Milly. That is the only reason I am putting up with you, Henry. Don't force my hand."

Days rolled into months, and each was the same. I scrubbed and polished the floors, rubbed and dusted the furniture, fetched water from the well, cleaned Harriet's shoes and boots, polished the silver, helped serve meals and prepared Harriet's baths. It was a far cry from playing with Harriet when we were children, but if she missed our childhood games she did not show it. "Pass me this, Henry," or "Pass me that, Henry," or other commands was all our relationship now. If her food was not to her liking she would say, "Henry, take this soup to Suzette. It is too cold, let her warm it."

Yet, sometimes I felt sorry for her, she seemed so alone. Once I expressed that thought to mother, but she snapped, "Your feelings are misplaced. Harriet does not need anyone's sympathy. She was born with a silver spoon in her mouth!"

Harriet helped me in an important way, though she did not know it. While her tutor was giving her lessons, it was the custom for a slave to stand by the door to attend to any need. As Harriet learned arithmetic, reading and writing, so did I. I learned the alphabet and how to put together the sounds to form words. I learned to read. I learned to cipher. And it awakened a thirst for learning in me. I would leaf through her reader, do sums on her slate, all while she was taking her afternoon nap, for there would be hell to pay if I was caught.

And I was. It happened this way. Simmons was going through some grammar drills with Harriet. Automatically, I was mouthing the answers, too.

"What are you doing, boy?" he snarled. "These lessons are not for you."

Harriet turned and looked at me. Her eyes were tender but she said nothing.

Mr. Simmons walked toward me. "How much do you know, boy?"

"Nothing, Massa. Nothing."

"Can you read or write?"

"No, Massa, no." I heard the fear in my own voice.

"I sure hope not. For your own good I sure hope not." Simmons looked down at me, his eyes mean and menacing. "Never let me find you mixing up yourself with learning. If you do, your master will put you to work in the fields. Or sell you down the river." And he slammed the door in my face.

Why was it that a White child like Harriet could learn and a slave child like me should not? "Slaves were made for hard work. Whites were made to manage them," David White often said.

In truth, it was dangerous for a slave to read and write and to display that learning. Slaves were often maimed or killed if their masters discovered they had learning. If slaves learned to read they could write passes that said they were free or had their master's permission to travel, and then run from slavery. They could read their masters' documents and come to know his business. They could read books that would open their minds to light and wisdom. They could think about their condition as slaves and take steps to liberate themselves. Literacy was a key to freedom.

A boy like me could be punished by being whipped and put to picking tobacco. That I could bear, but to be sold down the river, to be sent to plantations in the deep south, was certain death. Even the names of those places — Georgia, Mississippi, Arkansas, Louisiana, Alabama — struck terror into every slave's heart. It was said that work in the cotton or cane fields of the South could kill a strong slave in mere months. I had seen slave traders in Bedford town carting away chained slaves destined for the markets of Louisiana. A more heartrending weeping and wailing I had never heard as the captives were torn from their loved ones and their homes.

As I stood outside the door of Harriet's study, my body shook and my heart raced. I said to myself, "You have to more careful, Henry."

It was the Christmas season of 1825 and my master David White came back from the state capital, as the government had recessed for the holidays. Though no one really liked our master, his return broke the monotony of our existence. He always brought guests, and we took pleasure in making fun of them. Our master's personal servant was also a fount of information. Lord Byron knew every bit of gossip about the people of Frankfort. As soon as he had settled our master, he came to the kitchen and regaled the household with news. Lord Byron was from Trimble County like all of us, but in his eyes we were country bumpkins. To us he was sophisticated and knowledgeable. He travelled with our master throughout the state, and even out of the state. And because he was our master's valet, he dressed well, like a White man.

Before David White was to appear he would send instructions, so the house would be gleaming. My mother changed all the bedsheets, and supervised the preparations. Hogs and goats were killed and cured, and for days such a cooking went on!

I was in the house when master arrived. I heard the horses neigh and master's voice as he dismounted. "Lord Byron, come take my horse." My master bounded in, the house shaking with his voice. "Milly!" he yelled.

My mother was already waiting in the living room, our master's favorite drink ready on the table. She stood tall and neat in the uniform that she had donned for the occasion.

"No welcome words from you, Milly?"

"Welcome home, Massa, and merry Christmas."

"It is not yet Christmas."

My mother did not respond.

My master then looked at me. "In the six months I have not seen you, Henry, you sure have grown. I have a new job for you."

My mother and I caught each other's eye. A new job? Did that mean a new hire?

I was not about to find out because Harriet came bounding and squealing down the stairs.

"Father, father!" She rushed into his arms.

"My baby girl." The master hugged her tightly.

At that moment Suzette yelled my name, and I escaped to the kitchen.

"My God, Henry, where are you growing to?" Lord Byron was sitting on a sack of corn and eating roast potatoes and a big piece of ham. "Come over here, boy," he said. He gave my hair a tug. I could not wait until he told us the stories of his travels.

"Nothing like coming home after months of travel," he laughed mockingly. Then he said, "I know Massa is happy to see your mother."

"As the Lord is my witness, if you ever say that again I will smack you with this skillet." Suzette was standing over Lord Byron, her frying pan threatening his head.

He looked at me with a foolish grin. "Didn't mean nothing."

"Henry, take this to Massa," Suzette said, and pushed a plate of sweet cakes into my hand.

It was only when I left the kitchen that I realized how hot my face was, and it had nothing to do with the heat from the fireplace. Why would Master be happy to see my mother? Would my mother be happy to see him? Only later would I discover that my brothers were the sons of David White.

<hr>

At nightfall we all sat at the back of Shadrach's cabin — all except my mother. Lord Byron was holding court. "Frankfort has the prettiest women in the world, certainly in all of Kentucky. White,

Black and mulattoes. Ol' Massa sure seems to love them mulatto slaves. And the houses, they are big ... with so many rooms. You should see the governor's mansion. It is bigger than the president's house."

Shadrach who had done some traveling himself, said, "In Louisville, there are many grand houses."

"But not like in Frankfort," Lord Byron retorted. "Anyway, more important news." And he dropped his voice to a whisper. "In the north, in New York, they formed an abolition society."

Abolition? What was that?

"Whites and some free Blacks formed a society to do away with slavery."

"That can't be true," Pearl said. "Massa White said slavery will last forever because it is the way of nature."

"Well, in the north they beginning to talk about ending slavery. It is all over the newspapers in Frankfort, and all the White people are talking about it."

"Well, glory be," was all Shadrach said, as he stoked the fire.

"Now, I don't want any of you to repeat what I just said. Whites in these parts are afraid of this

Yankee society. If they ever figure that you know about it, they will think you are planning an insurrection and sell you south. Massa David asked me in Frankfort if I knew about the abolition society, and I said, 'No, sir, never heard of it.' And then he said, 'Good, Lord Byron. You are a good nigger.'"

I had always assumed his name was as natural for him as ours was for us. But didn't "Lord" mean God? "How did you get that name?" I asked. "Why are you called 'Lord'?"

"The same way you got your name, Henry. Massa David named me when he bought me."

"My mother named me," I said.

"Well, Massa David bought me on the Louisville docks. I was waiting with my mother, father, two sisters, aunts, cousins — everyone from the plantation. We were to be sent south. My old master had died, and his son did not want anything to do with running a slave plantation. So he sold every jack one of us to Louisiana. He was going to take the money and live in the north. Said he was going to study at a fancy college called Princeton to become a doctor.

"So I was sitting there on a box, when I saw a

book lying on the floor. I picked up the book and began leafing through it.

"That's when Massa David showed up. He looked at me and said, 'Boy, you can read?' I said, 'No, Massa.'

"'Then why you have that book in your hand?'

"'Just looking at it, Massa.'

"'I'm your new owner and I don't ever want to see you with a book.'

"Here I thought I was going south, but Massa David had bought me to be his body servant. But the rest of my family went south. We cried and cried. It was dreadful."

"But how did you get your —?"

"As I went home with Massa David, he said, 'Boy, your new name is Lord Byron.'

"'What kind of name is that, Massa?'

"'The book you were looking at was written by Lord Byron.'

"'And who is he, Massa?'

"'Lord Byron was an English lord. Of the aristocracy he was. He wrote poetry.'"

This made us all laugh out loud, because our Lord Byron could not read, much less write poetry. But it was common for Whites to give their slaves mocking names. Around these parts were many slaves named George Washington, Thomas Jefferson, Hannibal and Caesar.

"What was your name before that?" Pearl asked.

"My old self is gone, so my old name does not matter," Lord Byron said, almost to himself.

"But here's more important news," he said, his face brightening. "Attention, everyone." He clapped his hands. Lord Byron was born for drama, and we loved him for it. "Massa David is to be married. He has proposed to a Lexington belle, and I do believe she accepted his proposal. We will have a new mistress. Harriet will have a mother. And Milly will be happy."

There it was again, my mother's name connected to my master's. All the pleasure I got from Lord Byron's news left me. I felt a hand on my shoulder. Shadrach looked me directly in the eye, and said in a voice that only he and I could hear, "Never mind, Henry. Never mind. One day, it will all work out."

CHAPTER FOUR

Christmas

At Christmas season, all work was stopped for a whole week of celebrating. This was the time when the slave people had the most to eat, when they visited friends and relatives on neighboring plantations. In the slave quarters, the women cooked meal after meal. The men repaired the shacks and built new stools and tables.

Massa David was at his most generous. He bought candy for the slave children and gave brandy to the men.

Each Christmas, Massa gave out new cloth for us to make clothing for the upcoming year. This Christmas, Massa David had rough unbleached linen shipped from a place called Massachusetts. When Christmas day dawned, as was his custom, Massa David came down to the shacks and cabins to smile at us and accept our thanks for the new clothes. But he was in for a shock: not one of us was in that linen. The shirt my mother had made for me itched so much that my skin turned red. And I was not the only one: other people had the same reaction to the linen, so we discarded it. Our people decided that for this Christmas, they wanted to wear white, and by some miracle they acquired white cotton. How they did so remained a mystery, though I believe Shadrach had a hand in it.

On that Christmas day every slave was dressed in white from head to toe. Pearl and her sister wrapped turbans as high as a tower around their heads. My mother wore a white dress with a wide collar and wide sleeves. I wore a loose pajama suit.

When Massa David came for his Christmas stroll we were all seated under the big oak tree having breakfast. We all intoned: "Morning, Massa. Merry Christmas."

"What happened to my linen?" was met with silence. Finally, Dinah, the midwife, being the oldest, spoke up.

"It was the young people, Massa David. Young people nowadays! They got it fixed in their heads that white was the color this Christmas. They said that all the White folks would be wearing white. We old folks could not change their minds. They would not listen to us." And Dinah shrugged as if she and the other old folks were defeated by the young people. Our master gave a loud "umpf!" and stormed away. When he was safely out of hearing we burst out laughing.

David White had strict rules about Christmas celebrations. He would have his on the day before Christmas and we, the slaves, would have ours on Christmas Day. That idea had come from Captain Barker, who convinced our master that it was not good for everyone on the plantation to be celebrating at the same time. The Blacks could be planning an insurrection in the guise of celebration, and the Whites, being intoxicated and full of food, would not be able to mount a ready response.

In preparation for the Whites' party, Suzette, my mother and the other house servants worked nonstop around the kitchen fire to provide all kinds of fare for our master and his guests. The work was endless. They also scrubbed and polished the floors, aired and dusted the guest rooms, beat the rugs, hung new draperies, polished and repolished the furniture, and cleaned and aired the armoires. The field slaves cut wood, made and repaired furniture, slaughtered animals and cleaned the grounds.

Guests accompanied my master from Frankfort, but even more visitors arrived from neighboring counties for the Christmas party. We thought our master would bring his fiancée, but Lord Byron told us she had gone to visit relatives in Philadelphia. I must confess that I was excited because of the party, and for the first time was glad that I was a serving boy.

The house was lit by a hundred candles. The light danced on the walls of the house and on the faces of the guests. The women's dresses were a combination of styles from New York, Boston and France, and each woman tried to outdo the others in her choice of dress and style. There were gowns of red taffeta, bright yellow silk, cream-colored embroidered muslin and blue satin. There were dome-shaped, whale-boned and billowing skirts, and many dresses displayed "gigot" sleeves that were supposedly worn by all French women. Their clothing was complemented by pearls, ribbons and laces. But their hairstyles lacked the variety of their dress, being either piled high or done in finger curls.

The men, not to be outdone, were dressed in silk and woolen suits, breeches, vests and top hats. Though it was December and the leaves had already fallen, and the land was bereft of flowers, the brilliant colors and laughter created an impression of a summer garden with many-colored flowers and peacocks flitting about. In contrast, we the serving slaves moved carefully about in our white attire, silent and barely noticed.

I carried platter after platter of food to the huge table made for the occasion. Suzette and my mother shouted orders to the two young mulatto slave women hired to serve at the party. The servers were dressed in crisp white uniforms and white hats.

As some of the men drank sherry, they became

drunk and their tongues loosened. As I served one man a piece of cherry pie, he asked, "Who's your mother?"

"Milly," I said. She was walking across the room holding a large tureen.

The man roared with laughter. "Ah yes, Milly, the one James Bibb was sweet on a long time ago."

I hurried away, the familiar warmth flushing my cheeks.

Luckily, someone yelled, "Bring on the music!"

Out of nowhere Hannibal, a free Black fiddler, appeared with his troupe. Hannibal always traveled with an entourage of singers and players, some slaves, some free. The slaves had permission from their owners to perform with him all over the region. Hannibal struck up a spirited anthem. The White people formed a line, their hands holding the waist of the person in front, and danced around the room, laughing and shouting. Then couples were formed, and they danced the the jig and other popular dances.

After the dancing, my master paid Hannibal an amount so large his eyes bulged. He said a quick thank-you and made an even faster exit. Many guests, too, took their leave; but some had fallen into drunken sleep on the couches, and there they would remain until dawn.

With the party over, we commenced the clearing and washing up. Glasses, utensils and plates were scattered all over the rooms. Spilled brandy and wine and half-eaten food littered the place, which was beginning to smell. The hired serving girls also helped with the tidying, so the burden was eased on my mother and Suzette.

When we finished putting the house in order, my mother and I went to the kitchen and Suzette gave us a hearty meal of rice, beef, ham and collard greens. We ate ravenously, as we had not been able to eat at all during the party. Then my mother loaded up some food to take to the boys and to share with some of the other slave folks.

Exhausted, we walked hand in hand to the slave quarters. The air was crisp and fresh and a welcome relief from the heat of the house. Streaks of orange and purple were spreading over the eastern sky. Night was giving way to day, and the party had just begun in the slave quarters. Hannibal was playing the sweetest sound the ear ever did hear.

Throughout the day, friends from neighboring farms visited us; or, I should say, visited my mother, as I slept away the better part of the morning. When I awoke, the slave quarter was all abustle. Some of our people had visited relatives and friends on other plantations and returned with news. At nightfall, we gathered at the farm and began our celebrations. Hannibal played, his singers sang and we danced and sang along with them. There was such a merrymaking, feasting and good time. We forgot our cares and woes. We forgot that we were separated from family members whom we would never again see. We forgot all the abuse and insults and humiliation. I even forgot the scars that would forever remain on my back, laid on by Widow Beverly.

During Christmas celebrations, there was less surveillance by Whites, and slave people took this opportunity to escape. Trimble County bordered the Ohio River, a natural boundary between the land of slavery and the land of freedom. On its north bank lay the free states of Indiana and

Ohio; on its south bank, the slave states of Kentucky, Missouri and Tennessee. Along the river were numerous docks and wharves, from which flatboats, ferries and barges took Kentucky slaves to the deep south. Determined slaves also used these vessels to cross to liberty. No slave in the Ohio River region of Kentucky failed to dream about crossing to Ohio or Indiana and traveling north to Michigan, and even to Canada.

When my mother found time to talk with Lord Byron, Dinah and Shadrach, she would ask nonchalantly, "How many walked on water this week?"

"Soon," one would respond, "we will know."

But Christmas week also had its traditions of debasement. The Whites had their strongest male slaves engage in wrestling and fighting matches, on which they placed bets. They fed the participants whiskey and got them drunk before they stepped into the ring, to increase their rage and postpone their pain. The bout ended only when one was reduced to a bloody pulp. Sometimes, he even died from his injuries. If he survived, his master would ply him with more whiskey, have a doctor look at him and give him a small portion of his winnings.

David White owned two brothers, Tom and Josiah, whom he entered in a fighting contest on the plantation. A ring was fenced off in a grassy area. Horses and carriages brought slaveholders and their friends. The fighters came in wagons or on foot.

Tom and Josiah lived in a run-down cabin, worked in the fields and were known for their uncommon strength.

Tom stepped into the ring with a slave from Jefferson County. They charged into each other like two bulls. They pounded each other with their fists, stomped on each other, butted and kicked until blood flowed. The Whites cheered. Tom was emerging the winner, and though I was glad for him, I could not watch any longer.

After Christmas we learned that four slave people from a neighboring plantation had walked on water. When my mother told me, she prayed for their successful escape.

On the first of January, David White summoned my mother and me. "I am leaving for the capital in two weeks. Harriet will board at Mrs. Madison's Academy in Louisville. It is not right for a young lady to be in the country by herself." He said the latter almost to himself. "And you, Henry, are being sent to hire. You are leaving this evening for Shelbyville."

CHAPTER FIVE

More Misery

I hated leaving my mother and brothers, and the familiarity of the plantation, yet a little excitement rose in me at the prospect of a town. Going to a new place, even as a hire, meant that one was exposed to new knowledge about geography and the larger world.

My new master was a merchant named John Brooks. In his store on the main street of Shelbyville he sold all manner of dry goods, peas, corn, flour, dried and smoked meats, teas, coffee, sugar, writing paper, chocolate, roped tobacco, imported fabric, buttons, jewelry, fancy foods and wines. He lived upstairs of the store with his wife and two small children. His three slaves, Frederick, Antonio and Derrick, lived in a shack at the back of the shop. I took up habitation with them.

My tasks included filling sacks with corn, peas

and other grains, lifting and carrying, and helping Frederick, the oldest slave, with the weighing. I also helped Mrs. Brooks with the cleaning and preparation of food, and sometimes she left her two children in my care.

I did pick up some learning from Frederick as I helped him weigh and pack: counting, adding and subtracting. Our master and mistress did not seem to care because what I was learning made my work better, and that enriched them.

Though my master dealt in foodstuffs, I was always hungry. I would even be awakened at night by intense hunger. He was the meanest and stingiest person that I ever came across, even stingier than Widow Beverly. He gave Frederick cornmeal to cook for us, and that was what we ate every day, rain or shine, turn-cornmeal, a semi-liquid mush, sometimes with bits of carrots or chicken fat. The injustice became especially cruel when we would be working in the store and smell the delicious foods Mrs. Brooks was preparing for the family.

My mother had given me two suits of clothing, but as the months went by I grew out of them. They also became ripped and worn, and I did not know how to patch them. So I had nothing but a shredded shirt and a pair of pants too short for me and as shredded as the shirt. Mrs. Brooks seemed not to notice, although her two darling children were always well dressed. When the winter came I shivered in the cold. Frederick gave me an old blanket to cover myself, and that afforded some warmth. But my feet became cracked and bloody from the cold ground. At least at the widow's I had worn shoes, although she took them from me when I left her employ. At the Brookses' I came to believe that I would surely lose my life.

Mrs. Brooks had a habit of carrying around a "woman's whip," one that was not too long but stung as hard as any whip Captain Barker used. If I did the slightest thing not to her liking, she would give me several lashes and did not care where on my person the lashes landed. Once, she struck me across my head. I felt a stinging pain, and my left ear began to throb. Then I blacked out. When I came to, I was lying on the ground in the yard and Frederick was shaking me. From that day until this present moment, the hearing in that ear is diminished.

Mrs. Brooks seemed incensed at my light-skinned complexion. "White nigger, this will show you," she would yell. "Think you are White, getting uppity, this will show you!" as she applied lash after lash. Sometimes she complained to her husband. He would strip me to the waist and beat me with a switch made from hardened hickory. My skin became red and swollen, and I grew sickly. I had no thought in the world but to die. I came to hate the Brookses with a passion that raged the entire time I spent in that household. I also became nervous and fearful. Every time I was in the presence of Mr. or Mrs. Brooks, I became agitated. I could not concentrate on my task, as I feared that any moment I would commit some offence. My nervousness became so extreme that my stomach could not keep down what little food I was given, and I grew even thinner.

My only respite was on the occasional Sunday. Enslaved people usually had Sunday as a day of rest; but the Brookses gave us only every second Sunday to ourselves. We spent these precious free days in the woods around Shelbyville, making merry with slave people from the area. They organized foot races, wrestling games and corn-eating competitions. They played music and danced the "Heel and Toe" and "Patting Juba." Antonio won all the foot races, and Frederick, despite his age, was a superb dancer, who invented new styles of dancing and won great acclaim from the women for his skills.

But even those Sundays failed to make me happy. I would stand by myself immersed in gloom. None of the merrymaking could stop me thinking of the suffering that awaited me at John Brooks's home.

One evening, Frederick looked at me and shook his head. "Massa and mistress have no right to beat you like that. They don't own you."

"But what can the boy do?" Antonio asked.

"Henry is a hire. He belongs to his master. The beatings that the Brookses are giving him are damaging his master's property. If his master found out, he would be angry. No one wants damaged property."

Frederick seemed to know a great deal. He often travelled with John Brooks to Louisville to ship or receive goods. He was also much older than the other two slaves and had seen more of the world, having come from Virginia with a previous owner. A thought began to form in my mind. What if I could get word to my mother, who could talk to our master about the harsh treatment I was receiving from the Brookses?

But how would I get such information to her?

As if God was answering my prayer, one morning I was helping Derrick load dried peas into a wagon bound for the docks when Dr. Martin walked into the store. He was not a planter. He lived in nearby Newcastle and occasionally came to David White's plantation to attend sick slaves.

"Why, Henry, is that you?" Dr. Martin asked, as he came upon me. "My word, you have grown tall; but, boy, you look ill." Dr. Martin touched my face and I winced. "You have been lashed."

At that moment, Mrs. Brooks arrived and asked, "May I help you, doctor?" and he went to the counter to do his business. When he was finished he left the store without even looking in my direction.

A month later, Captain Barker strode into John Brooks's store. I was at the back peeling vegetables when I heard the demon Mrs. Brooks calling my name. Seeing the captain, I was seized by an overwhelming terror.

"Take your clothes off, boy," the captain commanded. "All of them."

I wanted to laugh because I was wearing rags, not clothes. Embarrassed, I undressed and faced the captain.

"Turn around."

I did as I was told. The place fell so quiet one could hear a pin fall.

"Mrs. Brooks, my employer, David White, has told me to inform you that the contract for Henry's hire has come to an end. When Mr. White returns from Frankfort, he will work out the details with your husband."

I could not believe my good fortune. How did this happen? Did Dr. Martin have anything to do with it? Captain Barker, who every day whipped some unfortunate slave on David White's estate, had appeared as my rescuer.

<hr />

My mother was standing on the porch of our master's house when I arrived. "Oh my God, oh my God," she sobbed, as she covered me in her embrace. After a moment she stepped back and looked at me, and the words tumbled out of her mouth. "Henry, how thin you are. Look at the welts on your skin." And she started to cry anew.

Some of the slave people nearby stopped their chores and surrounded us. Pearl cried. Two of her children had been put out to hire, and she feared for them, wondering out loud whether they were also being badly used. Lucy, the West Indian slave, disappeared and returned with some stalks of a grass in her hand. "Bathe him in water soaked with this," she said to my mother.

That night, after much welcoming and me making much of my brothers, who had grown so tall, my mother told me how I came to be released. Dr. Martin had told Captain Barker of my ill use. "It is not right that another man's property be so abused," was what the doctor said.

All the White men of Kentucky knew property was king. And slaves were the finest property. A man could maim or even kill his own slave, as it was his property. But for another to do so was cause enough to sue him. The captain wrote to

73

David White in Frankfort and told him of my situation. My master instructed him to make the proper inquiry and, if the doctor's words were true, he should return me to the farm.

"I don't want you sent away again, Henry," my mother said. "But for you to remain here, Massa must be convinced that there is enough work for you to do."

"I could work in the field," I said. Some people thought that field work was the worst of the worst because slaves worked for long hours in all kinds of weather. But I had been a house slave all my life and could honestly say that house work was as arduous. Moreover, the house slave is under the constant watch of the mistress or master, who can abuse the slave at the slightest whim, as I learned from Widow Beverly and the Brookses.

My mother did not reply. So I pressed on, saying that I was tall and strong for my age.

"Massa does not want you in the field."

"Why?"

"You are too white. It would not be right." There it was again. My complexion. "Captain Barker says that tomorrow you must go to the house to begin training as a houseboy, a sort of butler. Massa David is bringing home his new wife."

My master was away most of the time and had never needed a butler. Now he needed one, for when there is a mistress, a house must take on a more genteel tone.

"Will massa's new wife be mean or nice?"

"Only time will tell," my mother said. "At least Harriet will finally have a mother."

I had forgotten all about Harriet since she had been sent to her fancy academy in Louisville. Would she be happy about the arrival of a step-mother?

———

The following morning when I entered the kitchen I saw Elliot, the butler from Widow Beverly's estate. My face must have reflected my horror because Elliot laughed and said, "Don't worry, Henry, you are not coming back with me to the widow. I am here to train you." And he added the now familiar refrain: "My, how you have grown." It was true. I was almost as tall as he was, and he stood over six feet.

Elliot first taught me how to answer the door.

White folks enter through the front door; Blacks and slaves go to the back or the kitchen. I must always bow to Whites and keep my eyes lowered. I must say, "yessuh" or "no, suh," or "yes, ma'am" or "no, ma'am." I must always be polite. Next, he taught me how to polish the silver and set the table, to help serve the food and to anticipate the every need of my master and mistress. He also showed me how to be close at hand but not there at all. "When you are with them, as they eat, drink, talk, shave, you must be visible to attend to them, but you must be invisible at the same time. They must never feel that you are intruding.

"If you are angry with them, you must never show it. Smile, even at things you do not find amusing. You understand, Henry?" I nodded. "Whites do not like you thinking about them ... watching them closely. You must be their shadow, but they must never know."

I was thirteen years old. This sounded insane. How can I be visible and invisible at the same time? Slavery had turned the world upside down.

My training lasted the whole day, and in the evening Elliot rode off. Having his own horse was one of the advantages of being a trusted house servant of Widow Beverly.

And so my new life as a houseboy-butler started. I worked under the same roof as my mother, and that gave me great satisfaction. My brothers George and John had been apprenticed to Shadrach and were learning his trade. Only the baby, Lewis, remained carefree.

CHAPTER SIX

Our New Mistress

At the beginning of May, two weeks after I began as houseboy, David White returned home with his new bride. Her name was Phoebe. The day she was to arrive, all the slave people lined up in a row at the bottom of the veranda steps to receive her. We all wore our cleanest and best clothes. Because I was the houseboy I stood at the top of the stairs with a fan in my hand for her, though it was not hot. Everyone was curious.

"Wonder what kind of woman Mrs. White be like?"

"Hope she is not a tyrant."

"Nothing worse than a mean missis."

"Maybe she can prevent Captain Barker from being so evil."

"I hear she is very young."

Some of us said nothing, masking our disquiet. We heard the neighing of the horses before the carriage crested the hill between David White's plantation and the road. Soon the horses stamped into the yard and up to the house. My master alighted, his carrot-colored hair glistening in the sun. He walked around the carriage and opened the door. Mrs. White descended to earth. She was tall, almost as tall as her husband. She wore a sky-blue dress with a pearl-studded belt. Her hair, black as midnight, was piled high on top of her head.

Our master and new mistress walked along the row of slave people, and we all chanted "morning, Missis," "welcome, Missis," over and over. But she kept her head high, and looked straight ahead, as if we were invisible. She climbed the steps and reached the porch, where I stood at attention. "Morning, Missis. Welcome, Missis," I intoned.

She looked at me and her eyes came to life. "Well, wonders never cease," she said. Then she walked toward the front door with her husband. My mother held it open for her to enter her new home. "Morning, Missis. Welcome, Missis."

❦

The very day that Phoebe White landed at David White's plantation she took a dislike to me, my mother and my brothers. When John and George came bringing firewood to the kitchen, Phoebe happened to see them and asked who they were.

"Milly's sons," Suzette told her.

She flew into a rage. "Milly doesn't own anyone or anything."

She asked the boys to come closer, observed them. John had the same pasty white skin as her husband, and the identical red hair. The resemblance was unmistakable. She told them to leave the house.

After that, Mrs. White got upset every time she saw them, even from afar. She had banned them from entering the house, and turned her spite on me. I worked well to avoid criticism and punishment, but my work was never good enough for her. If someone knocked at the door more than twice, because I was not at the door right away, she would beat me with an old shoe. She had me polish the silver time after time even though everything sparkled. After my mother cleaned and polished the house, Mrs. White made me do it again. At nights, I was so tired that I wished never to wake up.

I had to bring the tyrant her breakfast in bed. One morning, she declared the tea too cold and threw it in my face. It was not cold; it scalded my skin. She also turned her wrath on my poor mother, who lived in torment. Nothing my mother did was good enough, and our mistress took pleasure in humiliating her in front of our master.

One evening, when master and mistress sat down to supper, mistress tasted a stew and declared that the meat was rotten. "How dare you think I would eat this?" she screamed at my mother. She then threw the bowl of food across the room. All my master did was to pat her hand and say, "Calm down, my dear. Milly will make something else."

Finally, things came to a boil between them. Phoebe claimed that a piece of her jewelry was missing and accused my mother of stealing it. She threatened to have her arrested, even sold. David White promised to buy her an even bigger jewel, but she would not be placated. "I want you to send that nigger from the house. I cannot stand the sight of her. Put her in the field."

And so Phoebe got her revenge. David White sent my mother to the fields. However, though she was not used to that kind of work, she saw it as a blessing to be out of the way of both master and mistress.

But Phoebe White was not yet satisfied. Next, she insisted her husband hire out my two brothers, his sons. And he did, to two farmers in LaGrange. Shadrach was upset because my brothers were making progress as apprentice smiths, and it broke my mother's heart to see her children scattered.

CHAPTER SEVEN

I Rebelled

I became angry and rebellious in my heart. I detested both my master and mistress and White people in general for how they treated the slave people. The abuse we endured in the house and the ill-treatment Captain Barker meted out in the fields galled me. The injustice rankled, especially as I keenly missed my brothers and I saw my mother's face lined with unhappiness.

All that Elliot had taught me about not looking White people in the eye dissolved as my true condition dawned on me. I began to glower at both master and mistress with hatred in my eyes. When I took tea to my mistress and she said it was "too cold," I would tell her it was not, because I had just seen Suzette pour the water from a kettle hanging over the kitchen fire. As for my master, I no longer polished his boots to shine. Sometimes I did not polish them at all.

Though my mother told me to desist, I could no longer pretend that I did not feel what I was feeling. I could no longer smile when I felt like crying.

I got back at my owners the only way I could think of — by destroying their property. One day while it rained and thundered, and lightning streaked across the sky, I broke my mistress's hand mirror. When she discovered it, she shrieked my name.

"You broke this," she said with confidence.

"No, ma'am, I did not."

Right then, my master entered and saw the broken mirror. "The lightning did," he said. "The large mirror in my study also broke, and I was there when it happened. A flash of lightning shattered the glass. I saw it with my own eyes."

I breathed a sigh of relief. I was lucky that time. But even such a close call did not stop me. I cut up some of my master's shirts, and once, as I walked down to the creek, I saw some bales of hay drying in the sun. Seeing no one, I pushed the hay into the water. Still I was not caught. At every opportunity, I did something that would displease my master and mistress. If Suzette was not in the kitchen, I'd eat from the plates and drink from the cups that my owners used. I dined with their knives and forks. As it was against custom for slave people to eat from the same dishes as their owners, I took great delight in doing so. Sometimes, when my master was away, I would go into his study and cut the pages of his books with a scissor. I cannot remember if I ever considered that my owners might find out what I was doing. I remember only that I wanted revenge and to fight against my powerlessness.

So there I was one day, cutting up the pages of my master's law books, when I sensed a presence behind me. I turned and beheld my master, staring at me with a look of utmost surprise on his face. He said nothing and quietly walked away. Still, I knew what was to come.

I went and sat in one of the plush armchairs that graced the study. I felt no fear. Captain Barker arrived, dragged me from the room as if I was a sack of corn and took me to the whipping post. He stripped me down to my shirt. Some of the slave people had heard what had transpired, and they gathered to bear witness. The women began to cry even before the captain applied the lash.

All my life, Captain Barker had been threatening to whip me. Now he had his opportunity, and I could see the glitter in his eyes.

My master stood beside him. "Do not maim him, but make this an unforgettable moment," my master said to the captain, and walked away.

It was, indeed, unforgettable, indelibly marked in my mind and on my back. After the eighth lash, I fainted, but the captain gave me seven more. When Shadrach cut the ropes that bound me to the whipping post, my back was a torn and bleeding mass. But it was not resignation I felt, nor was it regret. I felt only rage and hatred.

After my beating, I started running away again.

My master's shirt prompted my first flight. Mrs. White was giving a fund-raising party and her husband was to serve as master of ceremonies. He told me to take down his shirt for Suzette to iron, because it did not look pressed. I told him that I had seen Suzette iron the shirt the day before.

"Are you being saucy, Henry?," he shouted. I kept quiet because I knew his temper. "You have grown rude and insolent of late, and I will have none of it, you understand? Now take this shirt to Suzette for her to iron."

I don't know what came over me, but I remained rooted to the spot, my body shaking. I looked at my master's red face, and a rage came over me that I could not control. I shouted at him. "She ironed it already!"

David White was so startled that he dropped the shirt onto the bed. He walked toward me menacingly. Before I knew it, he was boxing my face with such force that the teeth rattled in my head. Tears spilled from my eyes, but he continued hitting me.

When I came to, in my mother's cabin, she, Dinah and Shadrach were bending over me. They told me that Shadrach had come to the house to bring Suzette some new knives he had made, when he heard my screaming and my master's shouting. He ran upstairs and pulled me from my master's grip. "Looked like he was going to kill you, boy," Shadrach said.

My body healed, but my spirit did not. I became melancholy. I had no desire to remain in the land of the living. But my master was not going to let his investment go to waste. Not wanting me in the house, he decided to hire me out once more. I decided to run away instead.

By this time I had some knowledge of the geography of my county. To get to the Ohio River I had to go through Oldham County, which bordered that river. I walked for a long time through the woods in the direction I perceived the Ohio to be, but I had not planned my escape properly: I had left with no food. I thought I could live off the land by eating berries, as I did when I used to run away from Widow Beverly. For three days I wandered, but there were no berries. I also lost my sense of direction, often coming back to the spot where I had started from. I became so hungry that I gnawed the tall grasses that grew wild. One afternoon, tired and hungry, I fell asleep on a grassy patch beside the river. I heard the bark of a dog in the distance, but I was too drowsy to rouse myself.

I woke up with Boxer licking my face. Standing beside him was Shadrach. He looked at me, his face serious. "You hungry, Henry?" I nodded. He sat on the ground and unwrapped a corn cake and some roasted chicken from a piece of cloth. I ate ravenously.

"Massa White sent me to find you," he said. "This is not the way to run away, Henry. When you are really ready, let me know. In the meantime, come on. Your mama is worried to death."

"What's Massa White gonna do to me?"

"Maybe hire you out. Maybe sell you. One thing's for sure. He will not keep you on the plantation."

I never saw my mother as angry as she was when Shadrach brought me back. "You could have gotten yourself killed. Massa David could have sent patrollers for you. You could have been killed by a rattlesnake." She boxed my ears, but began crying the moment she did so.

I was now a problem for my master. Slaveholders have one thought on their minds and that is to make money buying and selling slaves and earning wages from their labor. Many slaveholding families in the neighborhood knew that I was in the habit of running away. This made me a "bad example" to their slaves. Thus, my master could no longer hire me to any nearby farm. He resorted to putting a notice in the *Louisville News*.

FOR HIRE

*A mulatto boy named Henry. He is about thirteen
years old and is tall and strong for his age. He
was brought up principally as a house servant,
and can do all manner of housework.*

*He can also dress ladies' hair, and has some
experience working in a store. He can also tend
a garden.*

*For further information contact David White,
esquire, at Aurora Plantation, Trimble County.*

CHAPTER EIGHT

Louisville

One month after the advertisement was placed, a Louisville judge named Marson hired me to be his body servant. Shadrach took me to the judge's house.

I had not been to a city, and it filled me with great excitement. Never before had I seen so many carriages, wagons, horses, mules and donkeys jostling on broad streets. So many stores and houses made me giddy. People of all complexions rushed about as if attending to serious business. Many of the Black people were well dressed and walked with their heads high.

But it was the river that filled me with gleeful expectation. The city stood on the south bank of the Ohio. The river was broad and sparkling. Numerous boats, ferries and other water transportation lined its docks. The din that emanated from the harbor kept the city in a constant hum. As we passed the docks, I could barely look at the groups of slaves waiting with the dealers who had sold them down south. I thought of the great pleasure Phoebe White took in threatening me and my mother with their fate.

Beyond the docks we came to an intersection where there was an unusual amount of activity. Wagons were laden with Black men, women and children. Most were crying or emitting mournful sounds. White men stood outside a low, brown, brick building with whips and guns in their hands. Sad-looking slaves walked in and out of the building. "The slave market, depot and jail all in one," Shadrach said, without looking at me. "The slave dealer's paradise."

It dawned on me for the first time that there were dealers who simply bought and sold slaves, like any other commodity, rather than for their own use.

"Many Kentucky masters think they don't have enough work for their slaves so they sell them south to places like Alabama and Louisiana, where they have huge plantations growing cotton and sugarcane. Those places need more and more slaves." My excitement immediately left me.

We soon came to a part of town where the streets were broader and lined with big trees, and stopped the wagon in front of a mansion. A sign attached to the open gate read *Judge Alexander Marson*. Shadrach and I got down off the wagon and walked to the back of the house. I stared with amazement at the well-kept lawn bordered by flowers I had never seen before. At the back door, a woman looked us up and down. "What you want here?"

"This here is Henry. He is to be Judge Marson's new valet."

The woman opened the door wider and cocked her eyebrows as if to say "Come in." She led us to the kitchen. "Sit," she commanded. She dished out some mashed potatoes mixed with pork fat for us.

"Judge is still at court, but you may leave the boy with me," she said, after Shadrach finished his meal. "My name is Sarah."

"Henry, behave yourself. I will come back every so often to check on you." He thumped me on my shoulder in a friendly way. As Shadrach walked out the door, my heart sank.

"No need to be unhappy," said the woman.

"You'll be fine as long as you don't get in the judge's way. Just do as he says."

⚜

And so my new life commenced in Louisville. Judge Marson was of average height, but he had an imposing presence and a booming voice. When he spoke, his voice resounded around the room. He was a widower, and his two children were grown. His daughter was married to a very wealthy planter in Lexington. His son was a lawyer. He, too, was married, living in Frankfort, and had plans to run as a state senator. On the wall of his study, the judge had a framed document, which Sarah told me was his family tree. The judge claimed Russian aristocrats, English royalty, German farmers and French-Canadian fur traders as ancestors. Sarah often repeated that the judge was a direct descendant of a king named Charles the Second of England.

The judge had inherited the house from his father, who had also been a judge. Even though his children had moved away, he lived in the mansion alone with his slaves. Sarah, the woman who had received me, was the cook; Marietta was the housekeeper. Pierre, the gardener and carriage driver, came from Louisiana, and spoke French and Spanish.

In addition to dispensing Kentucky justice, my new master was one of the largest planters in the state. He owned a huge plantation in Fayette County, where he held more than seventy slaves. Most of its two thousand acres were in tobacco, but his slaves also grew vegetables, corn and hemp and raised numerous livestock. So large was his estate that he employed two managers and three slave drivers. Judge Marson also owned real estate in Cincinnati and a prestigious hotel there. He was immensely wealthy, and one of the most influential men in the state.

Much of what was used in his Louisville home came from his plantation: the wood used to make and repair furniture, the vegetables, the various meats; even the smoked fish came from a well-stocked river on the estate. But his needs were few, so he kept a small household.

I did the work of a body servant: I prepared his bath, combed his hair, cut his toenails and finger-nails, served his meals, shined his shoes, brushed his coats, and accompanied him to work. I brought refreshments for him into the courtroom, served him the lunch Pierre brought from the house, and recleaned his boots had they become splattered during the morning.

I, too, experienced the freedom Louisville offered its slaves. When court was not in session and the judge went to work in his study, I was allowed to traverse the streets of the inner part of the city. Sometimes I played marbles with other slave boys, many of whom, like me, accompanied their masters to work. Oftentimes, there were free Black boys in our group, and occasionally some White boys.

Walking along the wharf was one of my favorite pastimes. I loved to see the schooners, ferries and smaller boats plying the river; but in all my ramblings I avoided the slave market.

<hr>

The judge's place of work was the stately court-house, which stood overlooking the Ohio River. His office, with its dark, solid-oak furnishings, looked directly on the water, through huge French windows. The judge hardly spoke to me, yet I was to anticipate his every need. He smoked a pipe and the smell of smoke hung around him. I, too, soon carried the scent of the tobacco on my person.

I was the judge's shadow, and sat in his courtroom every day. I came to understand why my new master was called Judge Dread by all who spoke of him. He believed that wrongdoers should be punished to the full extent of the law and have no mercy shown them. Many who came into the judge's courtroom were slave people: those who had run away and had been caught, those who had injured their owners or other slaves, and those who had spoken impolitely or looked directly at a White person.

If an offender was a habitual runaway, the judge would sentence him to hard labor in prison and have the state compensate his owner. Sometimes he would order the amputation of a limb of a runaway or the branding of his face or shoulder. First-time runaways were given fifty lashes. Those who had struck their owner, or any White person, were sentenced to death. Incorrigible slaves could be transported out of the state to the deep south.

Judge Dread's courtroom was a forlorn place. Some slave people broke down, others fainted when the judge gave his verdict. A few stood defiantly, their heads raised and their eyes steady. After seeing the judge at work, I would return home feeling numb. One evening, as I sat with Sarah in the kitchen, she noticed my downcast look and said, "Cheer up, Henry, it can't be so bad."

I told her what I was seeing in the courtroom, and she shook her head sorrowfully. "Do not think about it," was her advice. She then told me that her family had been separated, too. "But I dealt with my sorrow by putting all my trust in the Lord. And that is what you must do, too, Henry. Put your trust in the Lord. There is a brighter day coming."

Christmas morning I walked into Sarah's kitchen and found Shadrach in conversation with Pierre. They were sitting on one of the kitchen benches, speaking in low tones, their heads bowed.

"Shadrach!" I shouted, delighted to see him.

The men looked up and grinned as if surprised at seeing me.

"I came to take you home for the holidays," Shadrach said.

I realized I had broken up a conversation that

they did not want me to hear. Children know never to butt in, so I merely said what was self-evident. "I did not know you knew Pierre."

"I have come to know Shadrach because of his smithing. He makes horseshoes for us when he comes to Louisville," Pierre said.

"Get your things ready, Henry. Your mama and brothers are waiting to see you," said Shadrach.

"George and John are back?"

"I went to LaGrange to get them for the holidays. All week I have been picking up the children sent out for hire."

<hr />

At the farm, John and George ran from my mother's cabin toward me as I leapt from the wagon. All three of us bundled into one another's arms, laughing and squealing. I had missed them so much. The baby was now walking sturdily and talking. My mother, however, looked tired.

Dismissed from the house by Mrs. White, my mother had been working in the field when Bedford's only tavern and inn lost its cook. The owner knew my mother's fame as a cook, and approached David White to ask if he would hire her out. The price must have been good, because my master promptly sent my mother to be the live-in cook at the inn. There she worked around the clock. She was allowed to take the baby, Lewis, although this was probably more for Phoebe White's peace of mind than any kindness to my mother.

Instead of the joyous family reunion I had anticipated we had a sad and lonely time. My mother was able to visit us only once, on the day of my arrival. We had a hurried meal together before she had to go back to work.

The owner of the inn, however, allowed my brothers and me to visit our mother there. We stood outside the kitchen door, or beneath the window, and talked to our mother as she worked. When the holiday week was over, our mother pulled us to her in a tight hug before we returned to our places of employment. As my mother's tears fell on my cheeks, I felt that I was drowning in a pool of sorrow that had no bottom.

During the Christmas week, I happened to see Harriet. She had come from the girls' academy and had brought some friends with her. I was helping Shadrach take firewood to the kitchen and saw them standing on the front porch, laughing as we passed by. "Well, if that isn't Henry," Harriet said, as if she could not believe her eyes. Shadrach and I slowed our walk. "Come here, Henry." I placed my bundle of wood on the ground and walked onto the porch. I was a head taller than she was, and she was by no means short. "This here is Henry," she said to her friends, "and I own him. I also own his mama and the rest of her boys." She laughed, and her friends laughed, too. This girl with whom I had grown up, with whom I had played, the girl who had stolen my milk from my mother, had grown as cruel as her father and stepmother.

"Are you done, Miss Harriet?" I asked her.

"Yes, go on. Go on with your firewood."

What would happen when Harriet came of age? When she turned twenty-one she would be able to do what she wished with my mother and her children. It burned my heart that we were mere things to be tossed about at the whim of our owner. Harriet's power of life and death over us fed my desire to escape.

Something else came to my attention that Christmas week. When Shadrach picked me up, the judge gave him my earnings to give to my master. The thought of working for wages and not being entitled to them made me angry. The money I earned should have been given to my mother. I had slaved a whole year, and had not the right to a few coins, not even a penny to buy a piece of candy for my brothers. They, too, had been laboring, and Massa David would receive all that they earned.

In the cart beside Shadrach, I was sullen and quiet. "What happened, Henry? You always have a lot to say," he said, trying to cheer me up.

"You giving my wages to Massa."

"Yep."

"It ain't right."

"I know."

"When you work for other planters, or for the racetrack, Massa take your wages?"

"I made a deal with ol' Massa. I get a portion of my wages, but I buy my own food and clothes. I am saving to buy myself."

"You get a portion of your wages? And you can buy yourself?"

"Yep."

"That ain't right!"

"What exactly?"

"You buying yourself. You have worked so long and hard for Massa. You made a lot of money for him. He should just set you free."

Shadrach laughed. "White folks not gonna do that. They want the money. They want my labor." Then he turned serious. "You know what Massa do with your wages, Henry?"

"Buy things?" I said vaguely.

"Your wages go to take care of Miss Harriet."

"What do you mean?"

"Miss Harriet is your owner, right?"

"Yes."

"Well, since the day you started working, ol' Massa uses your earnings to buy her boots, shoes, socks, ribbons, bows, dresses and the like. Whatever money you make belongs to her. Her father dotes on her and buys pretty things from the earnings of her slaves."

I was struck dumb by Shadrach's words. But there was more. "And now Miss Harriet goes to that fancy academy. Your wages and your mama's and your brothers' pay her school fees and her board. Help to buy her books and things."

"How do you know this?"

"Because when I collect your wages, and your

mama's and brothers' wages, Massa sometimes tell me to buy this or that for Miss Harriet. Sometimes, when he does his cipher, that is what he talks about. "John's wages will pay for Harriet's books. Milly's wages will cover her school and boarding fees. Henry's wages will buy her winter supplies."

I could not believe my ears. The knowledge that my entire life, labor and body were used to provide education and pretty things for another while my own condition remained destitute was too much, yet I had no choice but to bear it.

⚜

I continued working for Judge Marson until I was fifteen. My time in Louisville opened my eyes to a new world. When I lived in the country, I thought that all Black people were slaves; but in Louisville I learned otherwise. Free Blacks lived in homes they rented or bought with their wages. They were bricklayers, carpenters and butchers. Some owned stores or restaurants, and even inns. Town slaves had more freedom of movement than those who lived in the country. They went on errands for their masters, accompanied them on trips and sometimes were in charge of entire households. Slaves who had a trade oftentimes made their own contracts and found their own employment. Like Shadrach, some had agreements with their owners to buy themselves out of slavery. Sometimes, free Black people and slaves lived under the same roof. Some were even married to each other.

Corinthios, a slave friend of Pierre's, worked as a stevedore on the Louisville docks. He was married to a free woman who worked as a hotel cook. Because of his wife, Corinthios's children were also free.

Whenever Corinthios visited Pierre, they met in the carriage house and spoke in low whispers. Once, Pierre was brushing down the carriage horse when I took his supper to him. As I approached, I saw Corinthios bent over a table, writing on sheets of paper. He was copying something from a book.

"These passes look like the real thing. If anyone stops them, they will be fine."

"Let us hope so," Pierre said.

I stood outside for a minute, my heart racing. Then I cleared my throat and the two men practically jumped. Corinthios gathered up the papers I pretended not to see. Pierre looked at me, his eyes full of questions. But neither of us said anything.

So Corinthios could read and write. Maybe Pierre could, too. I marvelled at this, because to my knowledge none of the slaves on David White's plantation could read or write. What was more astonishing was that Pierre and Corinthios seemed to be involved in helping fugitives.

In Louisville, I learned where the east, west, north and south were. How the river flowed. In what direction the states were. The principal towns and cities of Kentucky and the region. And I learned more about the laws that governed slavery and the slave people. It was in Louisville that I learned of a network of people who helped slaves escape. It was Pierre who told me.

One day I was helping him clean the carriage when he looked at me out of the corner of his eye. He continued this behavior for a while and I finally threw my hands up in the air and asked him what he was doing.

Pierre laughed. "You sure is a saucy boy. No need to get mad. I was just thinking that you could escape if you wished."

My heart stopped for a moment. "Why did you say that?"

"During the nighttime, people would take you for White. You could go on one of the ferries and cross into Ohio or Indiana. No one would know you're a slave."

"And how would I do that?" I asked, irritated.

"You'd be surprised, Henry, boy," he said and remained quiet.

I was getting impatient with Pierre. "How would I do that?" I repeated.

Pierre looked around him, but there was only me and him in the yard. Yet he dropped his voice to a whisper.

"There are Black folks in Louisville who help slaves escape. In fact, folks all across Kentucky. If you wanna get north, you just have to be willing. Even the captains of some ferries help."

I looked at Pierre through squinted eyes. "If that's true, then what are you doing here?"

He laughed — a big and rumbling sound.

"Sometimes, boy, not all of us can go. Some have to remain behind to help. I can go if I wish, but I choose not to go, or at least not yet." Pierre remained quiet for a long moment, then spoke again. "Promise me that you will never repeat this to anyone, not even to your mother. You understand?" I nodded my head.

This was new knowledge and it filled me with hope. And yet there was something about it that was vaguely familiar. My mother was always talking about walking on water and of slaves who could fly. Shadrach, too. Did they know of this way to escape? Did Suzette know? Did Sarah know? Did the White people know about it? I felt that I had been initiated into some secret society with this new knowledge. I would walk the streets of Louisville and look in the faces of the Black people I encountered. Did they know this secret?

Yet sometimes I doubted what Pierre told me. I doubted because I would sit in Judge Marson's courtroom as he sentenced slave people who had tried to escape. Some had even crossed the river but were brought back by masters or slave hunters. Did these people not know of the secret help, or had it failed them? Though I had promised Pierre that I would not breathe a word to anyone, I told myself that one day I would ask my mother about it.

Judge Marson insisted that all his slaves have religious instruction. He was a Methodist elder, and his town slaves attended his church, sitting at the back. I could not understand how the Whites expected us to believe what the minister preached, that there was one God before whom all men were equal. They were rank hypocrites. They called themselves Christians yet abused Jesus' message at every turn.

I had little time to chafe under their lies, however, as my church attendance was cut short. This is what happened.

A poor White girl named Christina Drummond came to church services. She felt sympathy for the slave people, especially children put out to hire. Christina had a conviction that all people should be able to read the words of God; therefore, after Sunday school, she gathered the slave children to teach us our letters. Her instruction was like water to a thirsty soul. I did have the little learning that I had picked up from Harriet's lessons, before I was chased from her study, and I always wished to lighten my ignorance with more learning. Because I already knew the alphabet, Christina Drummond gave me more advanced lessons than the other pupils received. For two happy months we learned, until someone happened to pass the church one evening and found Christina teaching us. A gang of men descended on our little academy. Did Christina not know it was against the law to teach slaves to read? She said no, and that her only desire was that we read God's word.

Because Christina was White they did not beat her, but informed each of our masters as to our wrongdoing. When I got to Judge Marson's that evening, Pierre told me he already had heard the news, and the judge wanted to see me in his study.

He sat there smoking his pipe, the pungent smell of tobacco permeating the room. I coughed as I entered.

"I heard of your little adventure, Henry. How long has this been going on?"

"Just a few Sundays, sir," I said, my eyes lowered.

"Look at me, Henry."

I could not tell if the judge was angry. His voice was calm and steady. I looked up but averted my eyes.

"Can you read?"

"No, sir."

"God hates a liar."

"It is true, sir. All I learned from Miss Christina was the alphabet up to the letter M."

The judge sighed, as if he was relieved. "I believe you, Henry; but I am going to return you to Mr. White. I cannot risk having a reading slave in my household. Next you will be writing passes for your fellows."

I was not sorry to leave, but I had had a lot of freedom in Louisville and had learned more about the world than I would have at my master's. Nor was I beaten, and I had enough to eat.

"Pierre will take you. Tell Sarah to gather your things. I shall write a letter to your master."

As I was leaving, the judge called me back. In his outstretched hand was a two-dollar coin.

CHAPTER NINE

Walking on Water

At David White's plantation my brothers had grown taller but the manner in which they lived reflected the disruption of our family. My brothers lived by themselves in my mother's cabin. When I returned to the farm, I took up residence with them. Lucy cooked for them and had become their stand-in mother. David White had sent my brothers back to Shadrach as apprentices, and the smith, who loved them as he would love his own children, became a father to them. My mother visited them on Sundays, bringing food and love.

My brother George had a fine singing voice, the fact of which soon came to the attention of a White man named Samuels. He managed a singing and entertainment group of hired slaves that performed at balls, cotillions and other festive events. George soon found himself hired out to Samuel's troupe. I told my brother to take note of the places he visited because one day he might have need of geographical knowledge.

My youngest brother, Lewis, was now old enough to work with my mother at the Bedford Inn, and she surely needed help. Her face was haggard, and she was stick thin. She dragged herself around like an old person and sighed all the time. She would greet us in a distracted way, and her eyes held a faraway look.

David White had bought more acreage and had increased both his hemp production and his slave population. His wife had given birth to twin boys, and he was looking for a husband for Harriet. Everyone had a place except me. Like many rural planters, my master felt that town life spoiled a country slave because when they returned to the country they didn't adapt well. This was certainly true in my case. Life in Louisville had provided me with mental stimulation and increased my knowledge of the world. David White's farm now seemed a place of utter ignorance, where the slave people were like brute beasts, resigned to their fate. No prospects for hire presented themselves, and I would not run away until I was sure I stood a chance of success. But I was sure of one thing: I could not stay at David White's farm for long.

My master seemed to know what was in my mind. Whenever I looked around, he or the captain seemed to be watching me, and I had the distinct feeling that he was going to sell me. He hadn't said anything to that effect, but it was a common practice for slaveholders to sell their property without the slave having any prior knowledge of it. The poor slave would be doing his work, only to be suddenly seized by a slave dealer or his agent. Whenever White men came to see my master, I paid special attention, because if a slave dealer attempted to seize me I would fight to the bitter end. But that was not to be ... at least for a while.

One morning shortly after my return, David White called me out of my mother's cabin. I was surprised to see that I was almost the same height as he. I saw the flicker of that recognition in his eyes, but they quickly went cold again.

"You will be working in the tobacco field."

The other field slaves were happy to see me, but I felt a growing disdain for them. How could they live like this? My sullen attitude and superior air did not endear me to anyone. Worse, I did not know how to pick tobacco properly. I had been a house servant most of my life and had not developed the work skills of a field slave. But people kindly showed me how to do the work and in no time I became proficient. I then felt foolish and ashamed for thinking ill of the field workers.

No slave would challenge White people unless he was prepared to die. Slaves who ran away took great risks. As soon as their absence was noticed, masters sent patrollers with their savage dogs to find them. Slave people could not even be outside at night without a written pass from their owners. Blaming the slaves for their misery had been my shameful way of reckoning with my own powerlessness.

One morning in early summer, I awoke to the sounds of furious barking and angry voices: patrollers were combing the estate with their bloodhounds. The dogs bounded toward the creek, then stopped. They had lost the trail. This could only mean a slave had escaped. The runaway must have been from a neighboring estate and passed through David White's land. The dogs and their handlers came back to the slave yards and the dogs sniffed us one by one. Captain Barker told the slave hunters to search our cabins, which they did, knocking over furniture and throwing our few possessions in every direction. The dogs sniffed everything but found nothing to satisfy them, so they took off again, this time in the direction of the river.

Eventually the story reached us. There had been a scramble, a large party of slaves escaping. In this case fourteen had run from Franklin County and headed toward the Ohio River. Their destination was most likely Indiana, with the intention of going up to Ohio, and perhaps even farther north. All day we worked in quiet anticipation. We glanced at one another furtively. I knew that running away was fraught with dangers. Runaways could also be betrayed by Black Judases. Nature itself could be against the runaways. If they fled in winter, they would be at the mercy of frost, cold and occasionally snow. Sometimes they starved, or were attacked by wild animals. And patrollers with their bloodhounds, anticipating reward money, worked tenaciously to capture the escapees. Yet they escaped. One thought persisted in my mind: someone must have helped the escapees, but who?

David White said he knew that someone on his estate had assisted the runaways. Not one of us said a word. He threatened us with beatings and being sent down river. He bellowed and foamed at the mouth. Captain Barker cracked his whip.

Days passed with no news. Then, one evening at dusk I sat with some other slaves roasting corn when we heard the dreaded bloodhounds again. The palms of my hands suddenly turned cold. The snapping of the dogs came from the direction of a bluff that led down to the river. Moments later, two patrollers approached, pushing a man in front of them. The man's left arm was missing from the elbow down and blood dripped from the stump. He looked almost dead. The dogs were frantic at the sight and smell of blood.

The patrollers pushed the injured slave in front of us and hollered, "Let this be a lesson to you all."

The sight of the slave man's stump and blood made my stomach churn. I ran to relieve my stomach, and saw David White on his veranda with his wife and Harriet, dispassionately looking at the forbidding scene. Then, one of the patrollers clicked his tongue on his teeth, the other pushed the run-away along and the men and dogs moved off.

Shadrach broke the silence. "They caught only one. That means thirteen escaped. Good."

I could no longer eat any of the corn, but sat beside the fire, my head bowed over my knees.

CHAPTER TEN

Malinda

For two years I worked in the fields, each day crawling by like a tortoise. Every time I saw my master, I was certain I was to be sold. But that did not happen. I did my work and kept out of Captain Barker's way. But my spirit ached. Despair consumed me.

My life would have continued like this — a present without joy or satisfaction, and a future bereft of hope — had it not been for making the acquaintance of a young slave woman named Malinda. She eased the sadness in my heart and gave me hope to think that something other than slavery was possible. Here is how it happened.

Young slave men visited neighboring planta-tions on Saturday evenings and on Sundays. Some obtained passes from their owners for the Saturday evening outings, but many simply absconded and hoped their masters would not find out. The purpose of the outings was to meet with fellow young people and make merry. My friends often encouraged me to join them in their frolic; but I refused, having no heart for it. They persisted until one Sunday, having done all my tasks, I went with them to their meeting place, a neighboring plantation in Oldham County owned by a Mr. Gatewood.

In this manner I was introduced to the society of young women. And I must confess, it changed me. For the first time in my life, I came to be vain about my appearance, taking great pains to appear well dressed. I had always kept my hair long, and when I began to be attracted to girls, I pulled it back and tied it with a ribbon. I loved the company of young women and would do anything to please them. I brought them cakes and other sweets, and sang for them. I became a favorite among them.

It was during one such visit to the Gatewood Plantation that I met Malinda. Like me, she was a mulatto. She moved in the highest society of slaves and free Blacks. She was a businesswoman, selling her baked goods to both Black and White people. She was also what we called a "banker." A group of people would enter into a financial partnership whereby they would pool their savings, which were held by a banker. Once every six weeks, a member of the group got a "draw" of the amount that had been saved up. Malinda had the reputation of being an honest banker. She would not take one cent, but would be rewarded with a gift of money from whomever received the draw.

Malinda's mother had a head for business, which her daughter no doubt inherited. The mother had managed to save enough money to purchase herself from Mr. Gatewood, but was not able to buy Malinda; so Malinda remained alone on Gatewood's plantation, holding court among the young people.

I had heard that Malinda was of immense beauty. And indeed she was. She had red cheeks, a dazzling smile and dark pools of water for eyes. I was shy at first because she was surrounded by admiring young men, most of whom were older than me. I also felt tongue-tied. What would I say to her?

But fate intervened. One Saturday evening Malinda raised her voice in song — she had a beautiful singing voice. I knew the song and joined in. She turned to me and called me into her circle.

Who was I, and what was my name? Where did I live, and how come she hadn't seen me before?

To my surprise, Malinda knew my mother very well. I had never heard my mother speak of her, but Malinda's mother had come together with my mother from Virginia, and they had apparently remained friends. After we sang, Malinda and I sat and talked until it became quite dark and I was obliged to go back to my bondage. I could see that the other young men were jealous, looking at me with daggers in their eyes.

After that evening I became a regular visitor to the Gatewood plantation. All day and night I thought of Malinda. I would look up in the sky and see her eyes in the clouds smiling down at me. When I bathed in the creek, it was her voice I heard singing in the water. At every possible moment I was at her side. After some time, I told Malinda of my love for her. To my great delight she told me that she felt the same about me. One evening, a few months after our romance began, we sat alone together, gazing in each other's eyes. The tenderest feelings came over me, and I made Malinda an offer of marriage. She accepted.

Never before had I known such happiness.

However, an event was about to happen that would have an impact on my marriage proposal. Reverend William Smith was to hold a Revival in our area.

William Smith was a slave from Lexington whose master gave him permission to preach around the state. He had come to the Lord when he was fourteen, and had been preaching ever since. His fame spread far and wide and he was known to have converted and baptized hundreds of people. He even baptized some White folks in the Kentucky River, which caused a big controversy. The masters, thinking that religion would be good for their slaves, gave them permission to attend his Revival. Most of us from David White's farm walked the many miles to the meeting, which was held in a grassy field.

The Revival began with the singing of spirited songs. People danced and praised the Lord. Mournful songs followed, and then the reverend started to preach in a loud voice. He told us that there was only one God, and that God was love. He said there was only one Lord and master, and that was God. (I didn't think our masters would want to hear such a message.) Reverend Smith told us to turn away from our evil ways and prepare ourselves for heaven. "You can die any time," he said. "Would you want to die in a state of sin? Prepare to meet thy God!"

As he preached, I began to see the error of my ways. All I wished for at that moment was God's grace and forgiveness. When it was time to come forward to the altar for prayer, I was among those who made the walk. Tears fell down my face as I confessed my sins and promised to begin a new life. Reverend Smith prayed for us and asked if we wish to be baptized the following day. I said yes, and was among the slave people who were baptized in the local river.

Reverend Smith's Revival swept through the region, and it appeared that all the slave people had become believers. A great many of us, with the permission of our owners, began attending the local Methodist church. I had stopped going years earlier because of the hypocrisy of the Whites who attended. But in my condition of grace, I returned to the church with hope in my heart.

My master, David White, was an elder in the church. The first few Sundays I attended I was still filled with the euphoria from the Revival; but the humiliation of sitting in the "nigger quarter" of the church and listening to the White pastor preach about servants obeying their masters and that a good servant was better than silver and gold made me angry. I did not want any of my master's slave-holding religion, and I stopped going to church again. But some of the area's slave people organized their own secret meetings in the woods, with guards to look out for patrollers. I attended these meetings after I finished my work, and we praised and communed with God.

Though I loved Malinda with all my heart, my conversion gave me a new outlook on life. I felt I could not enter the state of marriage with someone who was not of a religious frame of mind. I told my fears to my sweetheart, who replied that for a long time she had been contemplating becoming a Christian and saw herself as a lover of God. I also told her that it was my wish to escape from slavery one day. To this Malinda also agreed, saying that she too wanted to flee. I could not have been happier to hear those words from Malinda's lips. We were in agreement on the two things that mattered most to me.

The following day, I rose earlier than usual and went to the Bedford Inn to see my mother. I told her about Malinda, and of my proposal of marriage. My mother objected, saying I was too young to enter into a serious relationship, much less get married. I told her that I would soon be eighteen, but she would not be dissuaded.

"Look at me, Henry. Look at you, and look at your brothers. We are all slaves because of me. Malinda is a slave. Her children will be slaves, too."

Her words hit me like live coals. In my amorous state I had overlooked that one glaring fact.

I left my mother more lost and miserable than I had ever felt before. That evening, when I was with my beloved, I told her that it would break my heart to father slaves. Though we would marry, we must try to escape. Malinda, too, had been thinking about the tragedy of bringing slaves into the world, and knowing that we were of one mind made me love her even more.

My master was not happy about my visits to the

Gatewood plantation. He knew of the object of my attention, but felt that the time I was spending at Malinda's was taking time away from his work, although he knew I visited Malinda only after I had finished my duties. The evil man threatened to stop me from visiting my darling, fearing that I would take his chickens and foodstuffs to give to Malinda. But I took matters into my own hands before he could carry out his threat.

One evening after work, I saw my master exercising his finest horse in the yard. I approached him and told him he was right — I was spending too much time at the Gatewood farm. I proposed a solution: sell me to William Gatewood. My master remained quiet for a while and then said he would consider my proposition.

A week later, he told me he would act on my advice. For a farmhand, I knew too much, and I had a reputation as a runaway. I believed David White would be happy to be rid of me, but he wanted to make some money off my person. Even though I had been a gift to his daughter, I was worth a lot of money as a grown man, if the buyer didn't know I had become "spoiled."

My master convinced William Gatewood that
I would be a good worker, because I would have a
wife to keep me in good spirits. My wife, too,
would be content, with a husband who would
make her happy. (It was Malinda who told me all
this. She was working in the house and eaves-
dropped on the masters' conversation.)

When I arrived at the Gatewood farm, everyone
knew that Malinda and I were sweethearts. We
approached the two oldest slaves on the estate and
made our intentions known to them. As it was
illegal for slaves to be married, we asked permission to jump the broom, a ceremony recognized
by the married parties and the slave people who
witnessed it. They gave us their blessings and
approval.

One Saturday evening, we gathered at a clearing
with all the slave people on the plantation. Even
my mother managed to come with my brother
Lewis. A broom was laid out in front of Malinda
and me and we made our vows to each other.
Then we jumped the broom, to the great delight
of those who watched. When we landed on the
other side, everyone applauded. The slave people

made a magnificent feast for us, and some of our friends played the fife and the fiddle. We ate, sang and danced all night. It was the best party I ever attended. Malinda and I were now married, in our eyes and in the eyes of the slave people, even if Gatewood, his wife and all the White people of Kentucky did not think so.

CHAPTER ELEVEN

My Brothers are Sold Away

After Malinda and I were married, Gatewood stopped her from working in the house and sent her to work in the field alongside me. One afternoon, a slave whispered that my mother wished to see me. That evening after I finished work, I walked the five miles to the Bedford Inn. My mother told me that there had been another reason why David White had been so willing to sell me.

Harriet White married shortly after I did. Her husband was one John Sibley, an upcoming planter from Oldham County. The wedding reception was a lavish one, held at a hall in Louisville for the cream of society. It was paid for by selling me.

Harriet had told my mother that she and her husband would be moving to Missouri in a week's time. Missouri was opening up to settlement and had become a slave state. It had become the land of opportunity for Whites, but another place of oppression for their slaves, who chopped down the trees, built the houses and grew the crops that made the White people rich. Three of those slaves would be my brothers. As for my mother, Harriet would leave her behind, in her father's charge.

I put my arms around my mother and she laid her head on my chest. Her cries came out in heartrending sobs.

⁂

I obtained permission from Mr. Gatewood to see my brothers off. Walking to the Whites' estate that Saturday morning, I tried not to think, but a thousand pictures crowded my mind: the slave dealers on the docks in Louisville pulling a baby from its mother's arms as they sold mother and child separately. I could still hear the blood-curdling screams of the mother, and shivers went up and down my spine. I saw the forlorn face of Suzette, brokenhearted because they had sold her away from her husband and children. Now the same thing was happening to my mother, to my family.

David White's yard was crowded with wagons of all descriptions. A number of slave people whom John Sibley had brought to his marriage milled about. I spied my brothers, looking lost, and my mother crying softly, standing away from the crowd. Shadrach was leaning against a tree, watching the scene.

I was determined not to surrender to the despair that was gnawing at my heart. I called each brother by name, and said, "Take notice of every place you travel. One day you will need the knowledge. Know in your heart that one day you will run from slavery. Do you understand?" Then I told them the story of the Africans who walked on water, and of those who could fly. My mother spoke. "My beautiful sons," she sobbed, "you will always be in my heart."

Shadrach entered our little circle, and embraced my brothers. "If I see you again in this life," he said, "I expect you to be free men." To each brother he gave a gift of money.

"Milly," he said, "I am so sorry." He paused as if to say something else, but thought better of it, and walked away.

We stayed embracing amidst the noise and sadness of other slave people crying and giving encouragement to their loved ones.

Harriet soon came out of the house with Mr. Sibley, David White behind them. At the foot of the steps, Harriet embraced her father. Her face was wet, and her father had tears spilling from his eyes, too.

Soon the cavalcade was on its way. Some of their slave people climbed into wagons, others followed on foot. My brothers, because they were young, were to ride. We embraced one last time before they climbed in. I, who had steeled myself to be strong, cried openly as they headed out of David White's yard.

———

I returned to the Gatewood farm and told Malinda of how my brothers were stolen from our mother. Knowing that we would never see each other again in this life made me more determined than ever to escape. I swore to her that I would one day own myself and my family, or die trying.

That night, after our work was done, my darling wife took my hand. There were tears in her eyes. "I am now certain," she said. "Henry, you will soon be a father."

I held Malinda to my chest. Waves of joy, sadness and rage passed through me in equal proportion. I was to be a father, but the father of a slave.

That night while Malinda slept, I went out into the cool, quiet night. Fireflies blinked their way through the darkness. I walked toward the grassy area that fronted the estate and the big rock that the slave people sat on for quiet recreation. The stars twinkled down at me. I heard Shadrach's voice loud and clear. "When you are ready to run, Henry, come and see me." Then Pierre's voice: "There are people ready to help you if you want to escape."

A smile played across my lips. Malinda was still mobile enough to make a long journey. Tomorrow I would speak with her, then go see Shadrach.

CHAPTER TWELVE

More Tragedy

My vow to pursue freedom met two setbacks. First, my mother fell ill. At the Bedford Inn she had met a free man, a fireman on a ferry, named Robert Jackson. After they married, Jackson went to see David White to buy my mother out of bondage. White said my mother was not for sale, but after several visits from Mr. Jackson he consented to sell her for one thousand dollars. Jackson gave him a down-payment of two hundred dollars and received in exchange a promise that, after he had paid five hundred dollars, White would release my mother. Jackson would pay the rest in installments. My mother's husband was in a hurry to get my mother released as she was with child, and they desperately wanted the baby to be freeborn.

The day after my mother's husband paid David White the last of the five hundred dollars, he died in an explosion. The furnace on the boat blew up, killing three firemen.

My mother went into early labor, and hovered between life and death. The child, of whom we expected the worst, was robust enough; but my mother remained deathly ill, with a high temperature. Sometimes she rambled and made sounds that no one understood.

David White learned of my stepfather's demise and came to visit my mother on her sick bed. But he was not there to console her. He told her that because Robert Jackson had not finished paying for her, she was still his slave; the new baby was also his. My mother argued that he had promised her husband to release her after the payment of five hundred dollars. But White simply said, "Milly, did I sign a contract with your husband?" and walked out of the room.

I visited David White and told him that, as he was not going to free my mother, he should return the five hundred dollars that her husband had paid. But he laughed in my face and told me that if I did not get off his property in five minutes he would whip me and have me jailed for insolence.

After hearing David White's refusal, my mother screamed with all the strength she could muster. The death of her husband and the treachery of

David White was too much for my mother, and she took a turn for the worse.

To his credit, Gatewood gave me the two days I asked him for so I could be with my mother and care for her. But when she grew worse I sent a message to him that I had to stay longer. He sent back word that if he did not find me on his plantation within twelve hours he would have me declared a runaway and imprison me. My mother told me to leave. She said she would send word to me if she got any worse. Luckily, Malinda's mother came to nurse my mother and look after the baby. With a heavy heart, I departed. I knew I could not make a bid for freedom knowing that she was at death's door.

As the time passed my mother's body healed, but I knew that her heart was forever broken.

Again, I contemplated my escape, but once more fate intervened: Malinda's brother died. He was thirteen years old. His mother had given birth to him after she had bought her freedom, although her two older children had been born slaves.

His name was Eric, a sweet boy, whose good nature and kindness endeared him to everyone. He was my wife's pet, and whenever he came to visit she made him cakes and special treats. Eric was on his way home from an errand when a group of White boys his age taunted him. Frightened, Eric ran away, but the boys came after him. The boys hated Eric, because he was freeborn. So they caught him and beat him until he was dead. We knew how Eric died because one of the boys confessed when questioned by the police. But nothing came of it: it was legal for Whites to kill Negroes.

Eric's death threw my wife and her family into despair. They could not be consoled. All the Black people in the area came to the funeral, as well as the few Whites who felt the injustice of it. I do not believe my wife ever recovered fully. After Eric died, did I only imagine that she walked slower than before? One thing was sure: she lost her appetite and did not eat for many days. I feared for her and the child she was carrying.

Such tragedies had struck our families that we could only mourn. A full year would pass before I would turn my mind again to freedom.

CHAPTER THIRTEEN

Flight

In the midst of our sorrow a sun burst into our life. Malinda gave birth to our baby, whom we named Mary Frances. She was our angel. From the moment she was born she was all smiles. She giggled and gurgled, and I was filled with a consuming love for her. Both Malinda and I doted on her. As soon as she uttered a sigh or cry of unhappiness we would quickly pick her up, feed her, sing to her or hold her close. As she grew she took on a strong resemblance to my mother.

Whenever my mother had time, she visited and paid every attention to her granddaughter. Malinda's mother treated Mary Frances in much the same way.

Mary Frances's birth brought a glow to our lives, but it did not prevent ill-ease from gnawing at my heart. Her birth showed me clearly that I would never be happy knowing that at any minute she and her mother could be taken from me, turning our lives upside down and plunging us into unending misery. I was in torment. I had to flee.

Night covered me like a warm and protective blanket. I knew every rise and curve of the land. Staring ahead into the blackness, I walked down the hill from the Gatewood plantation to a ravine that opened into flat prairie. From there the walk to the Ohio River would be easy. About a mile along the ravine, I came to a rock where I had sat so many times to dream and think and wonder; but now I walked with the hurried steps of a fugitive. As I walked I heard the music from the plantation recede. The slaves were dancing and making merry. It was my second Christmas on the Gatewood plantation.

I thought of my wife and child and my heart beat like a frightened deer. In my mind's eye, I saw my wife kissing our daughter, and gently throwing her in the air and hearing her squeal with delight.

I pushed the fear from my mind and focused on my task: getting to the big river and boarding the ferry to Cincinnati. In the distance I heard the hoot of an owl. My heart lurched and courage failed me. The full gravity of what I was doing crashed down on me. I wanted to run back to the Gatewood farm, run to my family and hold them in my arms. But a rage so strong took hold of my body that I had to gasp for breath. I left the ravine for the grassy savanna and the last hill before I reached the river.

The holiday had come with the usual festivities, the slave people getting and eating more food than they got or ate during the entire year. Gatewood plied them with liquor and allowed them to sing and dance throughout the night. I was sick of what I saw as my master's manipulation: a year of hunger followed by a week of feasting. And we, instead of fighting against our debasement, were grateful for the crumbs our master threw our way.

Even if I had stayed, I would not have been able to enjoy Christmas. In the middle of November, Malinda and I, along with other laborers, were in the fields gathering up the last of the produce. After Mary Frances was born, my wife had been allowed to stay with her for three weeks — a generous time from the point of view of our master. When a woman gives birth, she needs nurture and care to rebuild her strength; but slave masters expected them to be right back scrubbing their clothes, cooking their meals and toiling in the fields.

Malinda fashioned a sack for Mary Frances, tied it around her back, and carried the baby as she worked; but as the child grew and started to crawl it was no longer practical. Mary Frances begged to be placed on the ground, where she would eat dirt and leaves and often get stung by insects. Our greatest fear was that she would be bitten by one of the rattlesnakes that inhabited our part of Kentucky.

It was customary that the babies and infants were left under the care of a slave nanny while their parents labored in the fields; but the Gatewoods wanted even the old women, who usually cared for infants, to labor. Mrs. Gatewood herself supervised the little ones.

Mary Frances was seven months old when we left her with Mrs. Gatewood. When we fetched her after work that first evening, her face was stained with tears and she had dirt around her mouth. We took her home, bathed her and fed her. The poor child ate like a ravenous lion. We suspected that Mrs. Gatewood had not fed Mary Frances all day. Then, a few days before Christmas, there were purple bruises all over her face. Mrs. Gatewood's fingers were clearly imprinted on my daughter's cheeks.

"What is this?" I shouted. "What is this?" My voice echoed through the house. Mr. Gatewood, who was lounging in the sitting room, turned and said offhandedly, "Now, Henry, keep your voice down. The child just picked up a few bruises crawling around."

Malinda took the baby from my arms and broke into tears.

"Both of you leave my house and take your child. I cannot stand this racket." Mrs. Gatewood, the monster, had appeared.

"This will be the last time you mistreat my child," I said, and stormed from the house.

"Is that a threat, Henry?" asked Mr. Gatewood, as I descended the steps of the veranda. "I'm talking to you, boy. Turn around."

I faced him.

"Is that a threat?" he hissed.

"No, sir."

"It better not be."

⟡

Unlike David White, who hired a slave driver and beater in the form of Captain Barker, Gatewood did the driving and beating himself. He was not as wealthy as David White, and he was so stingy that he would rather torture his slaves than hire anyone to do it. It was also rumored that Gatewood had lecherous feelings for my wife, but she had not encouraged his attention. He was most unhappy at my presence, but took it out on my wife. Sometimes, he would examine our work and, of course, always found fault with it. Once, when he was exclaiming how lazy Malinda was, she, in a fit of temper, exclaimed, "If you don't like the way I do it, why don't you do it yourself?" The other field slaves fell silent; only the sound of the bumble-bees could be heard. We all knew that our master would not take sassing from a slave, especially in front of the others.

Realizing what she had done, Malinda walked to my side and took my hand. Gatewood walked menacingly toward us, his outstretched hand holding the whip. He ordered Malinda to take off her blouse and kneel. Right there in the field, in front of me and my fellow slaves, he whipped my half-naked wife, and looked at me fully in the eyes as he did so.

The instant he applied the first lash, I rushed forward with the intention of choking the life out of him.

"Attack me, boy," Gatewood said in a low voice. "Attack me, boy." But my fellows in bondage held me back.

Later that evening in our cabin, I washed Malinda's cuts and bruises with lemongrass water. We held each other and cried. I told her that the time had come for us to leave, that I would gain my freedom, and hers and Mary Frances's, or die trying. If I stayed much longer and had to endure the abuse of my family I would harm the Gatewoods.

For days I stayed in a sour mood, and my wife became afraid for me. She told me constantly not to do anything foolish. She knew that my heart raged against the Gatewoods, and that if I gave in to my feelings I would also bring harm to our family, because any Black or slave person who raised a hand to a White person broke the law and would be executed, if he lived long enough to be arrested.

Our condition degraded us, yet if we strove to end our degradation, we could be whipped, sold or killed. Nevertheless, the time had come for me to become my own master.

I went to see Shadrach at my old plantation. I knew this was dangerous because my old master had warned me off his plantation when I demanded the return of the five hundred dollars to my mother. So I went in the dead of night.

It seemed to me that Shadrach would never grow old. He looked the same as when I was a child, his smooth and shiny skin pulled tight across his face, his walk as sprightly as a boy's. Boxer, that faithful dog, announced my arrival, and jumped all over me.

To ensure our privacy, Shadrach and I walked down to the creek, with Boxer close behind. I told of my plans and asked for advice. Shadrach said the best escape route was through Cincinnati. He said my escape would be made easier if I told my master I wanted to go to work in the slaughter-house there.

Shadrach had friends in Cincinnati, and he told me how to find them. Before we parted, he reached into his pocket and pulled out four dollars. "Henry, you are going to need this," he said, as he pressed the money in my palm.

I thanked the good man, but was afraid to look him in the eye. I was suddenly seized with fear. What if I failed? What if I was captured? The White people had eyes everywhere to track down runaways.

Shadrach must have sensed my fear. He rested his hand on my shoulder. "Are you sure you want to go, Henry?" I nodded. "I need to hear you say it."

"Yes."

"Where do you feel it?"

"Right here in my heart."

"Then it is time for you to walk on water."

A day later, I approached my master with a plan.

The previous Christmas he had sent me to work at a slaughterhouse in Jefferson City, Indiana, just across the Ohio River from Louisville. The holiday season was always busy, and the slaughterhouses hired extra slave hands during that time. These slaves were paid a wage, which was collected by their masters. I had not been averse to going, because it freed me from the monotony of the farm work and the senseless carousing at Christmas time; yet it was also the time I could spend with my wife and visit my mother and brothers.

Mr. Gatewood had written passes for me and three other male slaves and took us in a skiff to Jefferson City. We worked there for two weeks and returned to the farm a few days after the New Year. I earned forty dollars, which Gatewood collected. Of that sum, he gave me fifty cents. My job in the slaughterhouse had been to drive the cows and pigs into a long narrow corridor, where they would come upon men who shot them in the head. Animals are not stupid; they can smell death. These animals knew they were going to die even before we herded them into the corridor. They bellowed and squealed in terror. It was the most awful job I ever did, and for weeks afterward I could not look at or taste animal flesh without my stomach turning.

So, before my second Christmas at the Gatewoods, I approached my master and asked if he was going to send me to work in a slaughterhouse. He was suspicious. "Why do you want to go away from your precious wife and daughter?"

"I hear they need hands at the general slaughterhouse in Cincinnati, and they pay better than in Jefferson City," I gave him by way of reply.

My master did not need much convincing. The smell of my future wages won him over.

"Come back this evening and I will write you a pass."

When I showed up later that evening, my master was in a sour mood. His breath stank of liquor. As he wrote the pass he said, "No monkey business from you, Henry. You not planning on running off, are you?"

"No, Massa. My family is here."

"Just remember that, boy. Just remember that."

Malinda and I had agreed that I would leave for Cincinnati the following evening. There was a Louisville ferry that stopped at Moore's Landing, four miles from the Gatewood farm. I would catch that ferry and arrive in Cincinnati in the early hours of the morning. Until my time to leave, however, I stayed with my little family at the knoll where the slave people were playing music, dancing, singing and feasting. It was festive, but my heart could not celebrate. I could think only of what lay ahead.

"Promise me, Henry, that you will come back for us," my wife said.

"Why do you say that, Malinda?" I asked, my blood racing.

My wife looked me in the eye and said, "Sometimes, people run away. They say they are coming back for their loved ones, but they never do."

"You and Mary Frances are my reason for living. I will not leave one stone unturned until I free you and our child from this pain. Yes, Malinda, I will come back for you."

I kissed her cheeks and eyelids. I smoothed Mary Frances's curly hair, thinking of how much she looked like my mother. "You will hear from me in two weeks."

"Just come back or send for me and Mary Frances."

The following evening, I stood behind the cabin with my family. In my hand was the small bag of provisions my wife had prepared for me.

"Godspeed, Henry," Malinda said, as she embraced me.

I gave Malinda half the money I had received from Shadrach, kissed her and the sleeping child in her arms, and eased myself into the purple twilight.

As I walked through the hilly country to the landing I was seized with conflicting feelings of fear, elation and sorrow. Then I thought of what my master would do when he found out I had run off. Newspaper advertisements would announce my flight. Slave catchers would be sent to find me. Malinda, even my mother, would be questioned. But I was determined to redeem myself and my family from the house of degradation, and I felt confident of success.

At the landing I found other folks — Black, White, slave, free — waiting for the ferry. Some of the slaves were traveling with their owners; others, like myself, had passes. Soon we heard the horn of the ferry. As I boarded, the captain did not ask to see my papers, as he required of the other Black and slave people. This surprised and puzzled me.

Then the light dawned — the captain thought I
was a White man. And a White man is a free man,
under no one's authority but his own. Under the
circumstances, being taken for White was certainly
a good thing; however, it made me realize how
slaveholders had robbed me of so much of my
African blood.

Though it was dark, I could still make out the
silhouettes of the round hills of Kentucky as the
ferry cruised up the river. On the south bank of
the river lay slavery; on the north bank, in Indiana
and Ohio, lay freedom. The cool river breeze blew
on my face and I inhaled deeply. Freedom! So
excited I was at the prospect that, although I had
rented a hammock for a few cents and that was
to be my bed for the night, I could not sleep. I
thought of Malinda and Mary Frances, sound
asleep. And so, with a thousand thoughts spinning
in my head, I passed my first night in freedom.

⚈⚈⚈

The following morning the ferry landed at the
Cincinnati docks. As I disembarked, I noticed the
name of the ferry, *Sea Witch*, painted in bright
gold on the side of the boat. I deliberately asked

the captain for directions to the general abattoir because I knew when my master realized I had taken flight he would have the ferry captain questioned. The answer the captain would give would encourage my master to believe that I had gone to the slaughterhouse.

However, I went in the opposite direction. As I left the docks, I passed a group of broken-down houses exuding foul smells. I walked on until I came to a clearing Shadrach had described. Three Black boys were playing at marbles.

"Do you know a small, old colored gentleman who lives around these parts?" I asked the group.

One of the boys, about twelve years old, pockets bulging with marbles, replied, "Oh, you must mean Old Dundee. He lives not far from here. We'll show you."

My heart was pounding. What if the boys led me into a trap? But why would they? They didn't know who I was.

"Not far from here" was a twenty-minute walk to a small wooden house at the end of a muddy street. All the people we passed in the yards were of the African race. This was Little Africa, just as Shadrach had described.

"That's where he lives." The boy pointed. And with that he and his friends sprinted away.

I swallowed hard as I walked up to the door and knocked. Almost immediately the door opened, and a man hardly taller than the marble-throwing boys looked up at me. He had piercing eyes and the whitest beard I ever saw. His first words startled me.

"You a runaway?"

I said nothing.

"Come on in. I can smell a runaway from way off," he said, as he held the door wide.

"Thank you, sir."

"Ain't no need for formalities."

I let out a loud sigh.

"You from Kentucky or Tennessee?"

"Kentucky."

"We have to get you out of here as soon as possible."

"I am supposed to be working at the slaughter-house."

"So that gives you about two weeks. In that time, we can get you to Sandusky. You hungry?"

"No, thank you."

"My wife will fix you some food. Eat it anyways. You'll need it on your journey."

As if on cue, a woman as tiny as Old Dundee appeared with a tray. On it were a cup of steaming milk, corn cakes and roast beef.

I took the tray and murmured my thanks.

"Eat while I get the wagon," said Old Dundee.

Though I was too anxious to be hungry, I ate the meal with relish. As soon as I put the last morsel in my mouth, Old Dundee yelled from outside, "Let's get going!" I thanked Mrs. Dundee and joined my savior outside.

For a week I stayed hidden in the home of a Black Methodist preacher and his family in North Cincinnati, while arrangements were being made to get me to Sandusky, Ohio. The plan was for me to travel from there to Adrian, Michigan, and then to Detroit. I could either stay in Detroit or put the United States completely behind me and continue overland to Canada. Another alternative was to travel across the Detroit River into Windsor, Upper Canada. The day I was to leave, Old Dundee came to bid me farewell. With him were two runaways, a man and woman, with whom I would travel. He shook our hands and bade us Godspeed.

The night before my departure, I sat with the pastor and wrote a letter to Malinda.

My dear wife,

You are in my heart day and night. I think only of you and our daughter.

I kiss both of you a thousand times. I am safe and on my way to freedom.

Hold fast to hope. I intend to work throughout the winter, as my friends here advised me, and at the end of it will come back for you and our precious child. If I am unable to come myself, I will send another. I pray God to hold you in the palm of his hand. You are the reason for my existence. Know that if things do not go as planned, and if we do not meet again on this earth, we shall meet in heaven. I close with all the love in my heart.

Your loving and dutiful husband,

Henry Bibb

As I jumped into the wagon, the pastor reassured me. "I will get the letter to your wife, Henry. You can count on me. I have been helping fugitives now for more than ten years."

I nodded, and we shook hands. His wife and children waved as the wagon moved out of the yard. A Black man who transported dry goods between Cincinnati and Cleveland was our driver. He had carried human cargo north many times.

***

It was January 1838. The two weeks I was to work at the abattoir were over. My master would have expected my return three days ago. When I did not show up, he would cross to Cincinnati to look for me. And when he could not find me, he would take out ads in the newspapers and hire a slave catcher. He would question my wife, all my relations and everyone on his farm.

And no one would be able to tell him anything. I focused on the road ahead. The road to liberty.

Epilogue

Henry Bibb was successful in his escape; but, true to his word, he returned to rescue his family. Betrayed and caught five times, he was finally sold into Texas and never saw his wife and child again.

His final escape, in 1841, took him from Texas to Detroit. There, Bibb devoted himself to ending slavery and campaigning for Black civil rights. Michigan audiences clamored to hear a speaker who had had direct experience of slavery, and Bibb was a dramatic lecturer. Soon he was touring New England and the Midwest, narrating his personal experiences of slavery's barbarism. Newspaper accounts note that he often moved his audience to tears.

Bibb also remained a practicing Christian throughout his life, and held that slaveholders deliberately kept slaves in ignorance by denying them religious instruction and keeping them illiterate. With that in mind, Bibb raised funds to buy Bibles to distribute to slave families in the south and to free Blacks in the north.

In 1848, the publication of his autobiography, *Narrative of the Life and Adventures of Henry Bibb, an American Slave*, made Bibb a household name. The book was an instant success and was published in the United States and Europe.

In September 1850, the American Congress passed the Fugitive Slave Law, which gave owners the right to track down and recapture fugitive slaves living in the free states and elsewhere. Knowing that their safety was once again in jeopardy, thousands of ex-slaves fled to Canada, Mexico, the West Indies and even Africa. Most, including Bibb, came to Canada West, now Ontario, where there was a burgeoning refugee community: hundreds of fugitives were arriving at the Windsor border every day, and many needed help.

Bibb urged refugees to come "to the Queen's country," but also spoke out against the prejudice the Black people encountered in Canada. He urged Black communities to organize themselves, get an education, and purchase land as a way to fight racial prejudice.

Henry Bibb founded literary, antislavery and debating societies; he also established churches and schools in Ontario. He used the Sunday school movement to educate adults. However, perhaps his most lasting contribution to the Canadian Black freedom movement was the founding of *The Voice of the Fugitive*, Canada's first Black newspaper. The first issue of the *Voice* rolled off the press on 1 January 1851. It was dedicated to antislavery, universal education and social reform.

Bibb would gather some of the information for his newspaper by meeting the boats crossing from Detroit to Canada at Windsor, and interviewing the disembarking fugitive slaves. One day he approached two young arrivals, only to discover that they were his brothers, John and George, whom he had last seen as children. Their other brother, Lewis, arrived later that day. All three went to live with their mother, whose rescue and arrival in Windsor Henry had arranged earlier.

Bibb died on 1 August 1854, after a long illness. He was declared a Person of National Historic Significance by the Government of Canada in 2005.

DATE DUE

FOLLETT

Saint Louis Country D.
101 North Warson
St. Louis, Missouri